HARPER

AT FIRST *Sight*

THE PINK BEAN SERIES

BOOK TEN

Other Harper Bliss Books

A Breathless Place
If You Kiss Me Like That
Two Hearts Trilogy
Next in Line for Love
A Lesson in Love
Life in Bits (with T.B. Markinson)
A Swing at Love (with Caroline Bliss)
No Greater Love than Mine
Once Upon a Princess (with Clare Lydon)
In the Distance There Is Light
The Road to You
Seasons of Love
Release the Stars
Once in a Lifetime
At the Water's Edge
The French Kissing Series
High Rise (The Complete Collection)

the Pink Bean Series

More than Words
Crazy for You
Love without Limits
No Other Love
Water under Bridges
This Foreign Affair
Everything Between Us
Beneath the Surface
No Strings Attached

Published by Ladylit Publishing – a division of Q.P.S. Projects Limited - Hong Kong
ISBN-13 978-988-74416-1-8

Chapter One

Jill took a deep breath and opened the door. It had been a while since she'd welcomed a new client. Despite decades of experience, a ripple of nerves coursed through her.

There were two women in the waiting area, but she recognized the blonde as one of Patrick's clients. The one with the long dark hair would be for her then. Both women glanced at her.

"Amelia?" Jill said.

The dark-haired woman drew her lips into a smile and rose. Without saying anything, she followed Jill into the office.

"Please, sit down," Jill said. "Make yourself comfortable." She pointed at the chair opposite her own.

While Amelia settled in, Jill grabbed a notepad and pen from her desk, giving her new client some time to acclimate to her new surroundings.

A reassuring smile on her lips, Jill turned and sat. "Because this is your first session, I'll be making more notes than I usually would. Please don't be put off by that, it's mostly for admin reasons. Or if you'd rather I didn't, I'll try to exercise my memory and make the notes after you leave." She broadened her smile and took the opportunity to let her gaze linger on her new client's eyes. Deep-brown and rather captivating. Jill found it hard to look away from them.

"That's fine," Amelia said. These were the first words she'd spoken and if her eyes were arresting, her voice was even more so. Husky and low, like a soft and soothing bass note.

A tingle of heat crept up Jill's neck. This was not a normal reaction to a first session with a new client. Jill forced herself to look down at her notepad.

"Do you want to tell me a little about yourself or would you like me to go first?" she asked. "Either is fine." She looked back up at Amelia.

"You go first." Amelia's face was all tightness. She was probably nervous. In all her years as a psychiatrist, Jill had never encountered a new client who wasn't a bundle of nerves during their first session. Seeking therapy was a big step for most people. One they'd often already put off for a long time.

"Sure." Jill rested the pen and the notepad on her knees. "I'm Jill." Way to state the obvious. "I'm here to help you with whatever it is you want or need to discuss. Absolutely nothing is taboo in this office. This is your safe space. Nothing you say will shock me. I've been doing this for a very long time and helping people through a difficult time in their life is my passion. It's what I do. Apart from a couple of obvious exceptions, there is complete confidentiality between us. I can tell you about those exceptions if you wish."

Amelia shook her head.

"But otherwise, nothing you say will ever leave this room." Jill followed up with another smile. This was the moment to make the client feel a touch more comfortable. She discreetly glanced over Amelia's body to see if any tension was leaving her muscles. Apparently not just yet. Some clients needed to unload before they could relax. "I'm here for you, Amelia. I have your GP's referral, but I'd like to hear your reasons for coming to see me in your own words." Jill caught herself being a bit too eager to hear Amelia's voice again. She waited with increased anticipation.

"I—uh," Amelia started. "I had a burnout." She swallowed. "Very 'of the times', I know. I'm usually never up with the latest trends, yet here I am."

A rather dark and self-deprecating sense of humor, Jill thought, but didn't write down. She wanted Amelia to talk freely before she took any formal notes. Jill sent her another encouraging smile.

"About a month ago, I had a massive panic attack at work. I thought it would pass after some rest. I took a few days off. But as soon as I got stuck in again, the panic returned." Amelia put a hand over her sternum. "Since then, I've had this continuous agitated sensation right here. I just… I can't shake it. I can't relax any longer. I have no energy. I had to drag myself over here. It's been… utterly grueling because I hardly recognize myself."

"What do you do for work?"

"I'm a biochemical researcher for a pharmaceutical company. My team and I develop new drugs." She scoffed. "But as far as I know, no drug has been invented to change the way I feel."

"Is it a very high-pressure environment?" Jill asked.

"You could say that." Amelia sighed. "I know I need to talk about my work but even thinking about it makes me feel exhausted."

"It's all right. We don't have to talk about your work right now." Jill positioned the notepad in front of her. "Is it okay if I take a few notes now?" She waited for Amelia's nod. "What else do you do beside work? Do you have a partner? A family?"

"I'm single." It seemed Amelia's voice had dropped into an even lower register.

Jill hoped to figure out later if that meant anything. For now, she just listened and jotted down some short sentences.

"I was a cliché: the employee who turns the lights on in the morning and switches them off in the evening. I used to be utterly obsessed with my job. I actually loved it because I felt as though what I did mattered, but, along the way, I seem to have lost that conviction and now I feel like just another cog in the wheel of Big Pharma."

"What changed?" Jill asked.

For the first time, a small smile played on Amelia's lips. However tiny it was, Jill still thought it a beautiful sight to behold. She shoved that unprofessional thought away. She had just promised Amelia that she would be there for her and that she would help her. Being entranced by a hint of a smile was not going to further that goal. She'd need to give herself a stern talking-to later.

"Here I am, talking about work regardless," Amelia said.

"Considering you suffered a burnout, I'd say that's why you're here."

The side of Amelia's lips tilted into a crooked grin, the sight of which sparked a new tingle of heat to ignite in Jill's chest.

Oh, good gracious god. Jill wondered if she should ask for a moment to gather herself. What was happening? Who was this woman? She was a new client with a burnout. She was someone who needed Jill's help, for crying out loud. So why was Jill getting so worked up about the degree at which her lips slanted when she half-smiled? She should make a note to discuss this with her own therapist tomorrow. Vic would surely give her an earful.

"To answer your earlier question." Amelia's low voice pulled Jill back to earth. "I don't have a family. I don't have the best relationship track record. It's just not something I've ever been overly interested in." She just shrugged as though her relationship status was the least of her worries. It probably was. "Meanwhile, I think my biological clock has ticked past my eggs' use-by date."

Jill uttered the tiniest of chuckles while she looked at her notepad. She'd copied the information she'd gotten in the GP's referral. Amelia Shaw was forty-five. She was one of those women who looked neither young nor old. Maybe she just looked her age. Either way, there was something about her that had Jill much more intrigued than she'd been with any of her clients in a long time. She didn't consider this a good thing at all.

"No wish for a child?" Jill inquired.

Amelia just shrugged again.

Jill looked forward to finding out if this was her genuine attitude toward relationships and children, two of the key factors in most people's lives. Amelia was either very good at pretending, or had adopted this apathetic stance subconsciously over time for another reason. That was also the thing with a new client: there was still so much to discover. Jill's interest was piqued. Professional curiosity. The challenge of figuring out a brand-new-to-her person. The intricate puzzle of their personality and how it first presented itself. A woman like Amelia was one of the reasons Jill loved her job so much. Although in Amelia's case, it seemed it wasn't just Jill's professional interest that was piqued.

"I don't have any children," Jill said, which was true, although it didn't mean she had never tried to have them.

Amelia simply nodded. She didn't appear to be one of those clients who liked asking questions. She was here for herself. She hadn't come to deflect the attention away from her which was a technique many a new client tried. Jill was very skilled at gently diverting personal questions right back at reluctant clients.

"Do you have any hobbies?" Jill asked. "Something that takes your mind off work?"

"I'm the goalkeeper for the Darlinghurst Darlings." It was the first time Jill detected some genuine animation in Amelia's voice.

"Soccer?" Although Jill had lived in Sydney for more than ten years, most of them in Darlinghurst, she had never heard of the Darlinghurst Darlings.

"Yep. I take immense pride in keeping a clean sheet."

Jill arched up an eyebrow.

"Not letting the other team score," Amelia clarified. "Although my spot on the team is in danger, now that I'm in my forties. I'm the oldest player on the team—even, I think, in the league. You could say I'm holding on to something that I should let go of. You know, give someone younger a chance, but it's hard for me… That team is like my family, even though most of the women I started out playing with have long stopped. And I will admit it's not always easy keeping up with the younger ones." She puffed up her cheeks and blew out some air. "Then again, as the goalkeeper, I don't have to run that much during a game."

Amelia's precarious spot on the team might have contributed to her work burnout. Jill jotted another note.

"Sounds like a fun hobby."

"I love it… I've been thinking about starting a league for 40+ women, but the pickings are slim. Turns out women in their forties have other things to do in their spare time than play soccer." She narrowed her eyes. "How old are you, if I may ask?"

Jill burst out into a chuckle, although, these days, she

didn't particularly enjoy being asked about her age. "Forty-nine."

"Do you play any sport?" Amelia sure was passionate about this topic.

"I'm, um, more of an art aficionado," Jill heard herself say. Could she sound any more pretentious?

"Oh, well, I guess I shouldn't consider you for my mature players' league then." Amelia's lips stretched into the most glorious smile Jill had witnessed for as long as she could remember. The thought that she'd be willing to try soccer for Amelia flashed through her mind but she managed to extinguish it as soon as she identified it as utterly foolish.

Chapter Two

Ever since her first panic attack, whenever Amelia felt stressed or anxious, she focused her thoughts on soccer. Because for as long as she could remember, the pitch had been her happy place. Talking about soccer with her new therapist helped to alleviate that crushing feeling in her chest and was easier than talking about the real cause for her burnout.

Although, perhaps, she shouldn't have tried to recruit her therapist for the 40+ league that didn't even exist yet. She could have also guessed that Jill wasn't one for rowdy sport, although you just never knew. Some of the women she played with were unrecognizable to Amelia when they were dressed in office attire.

"I wouldn't be much of an asset," Jill said. She was smiling again. "I've never kicked a ball in my life."

This was Amelia's first experience with a therapist and she hadn't expected her to smile so much. Maybe she just wanted to put Amelia at ease. It was kind of working, although Amelia was still pretty nervous.

"If you know anyone in our age group from the neighborhood who would be interested…" Amelia inwardly scolded herself for not letting this go. On the other hand, Jill must have heard people say far worse things. Especially first-timers who didn't really know where to begin.

"Sure." The skin around Jill's eyes crinkled. She surely had one thing going for her as a therapist: the woman oozed kindness. It was etched into her face somehow. Or maybe that's what happens when it's your job to listen to people's worries all day long. Your face adapts. That soothing expression becomes permanent. Amelia wondered if any studies had been done about that. She made a mental note to go on Google Scholar later… Argh, no. No looking up any academic research. Amelia was on leave. But it was hard to totally switch off her scientific brain.

"It, um," Amelia started again. She'd beaten around the bush long enough. "It seems I have a very difficult time relaxing." She chuckled nervously. "Even on the pitch I'm always doing some sort of calculation to try and predict where the ball will go next." She shook her head. "I know it sounds a little nuts. Obsessive even." Another chuckle. "I guess that's why I'm here."

"Is it possible to make such a prediction? I thought soccer was mostly a game of chance?"

Amelia frowned. "Whoever told you that doesn't know the first thing about soccer. I mean, sure, chance and luck have a great deal to do with it, but I would say definitely no more than 50% of the game is down to chance. Technique is very important as is physical condition and of course so is the composition of the team. I wouldn't say—" Amelia caught herself. She was waffling on, trying to drive home a point that had no importance in this conversation. Although on this particular subject she knew for certain that a scientific study had been done. She'd pored over it with great interest.

"It's mainly me who doesn't know the first thing about soccer." Jill wrote something down again.

Amelia shuffled in her chair. It was a slightly disconcerting thing to witness—someone making notes about her.

"Whenever I have a pressing question about it in the future, I'll know who to call from now on." Jill grinned at her.

"I'm sorry. I get quite passionate about the whole thing. My life used to totally revolve around work, but now it seems that soccer has taken its place. I'm on sick leave, which I utterly despise. I want to work, but... I can't. It makes me feel so powerless."

"It's completely normal to feel this way, Amelia." Jill paused. "In a way, it's good that you have soccer to turn to."

"Due to my low energy levels, I've missed more than a few practices and let's just say it's not that difficult to replace me on the team."

"Would it be fair to say that you're currently feeling like everything's slipping away from you?"

"I think that would be a pretty accurate assessment." Now that she was a good while into her first session, the burst of adrenaline that had brought her there seeped from her body. Against her will, she heaved a big sigh. "I'm sorry." Her voice broke a little. "I'm such a mess. I don't even know where to begin to fix this."

"You've already begun," Jill said. "You're here. Coming to me was the hard part. I've got your back now."

Amelia summoned every ounce of willpower she could to hold back the tears gathering behind her eyes. She wasn't the crying type—at least not until she'd crashed at work with her first panic attack. Oh, the shame of going through that mortifying ordeal in front of her co-workers. At first, she believed she was having a heart attack, despite all the scientific evidence pointing to the contrary. She'd had blood work done only a few weeks prior and her physical health was optimal for her age. There were no indications for any cardiovascular disease in her body, no matter the hours she worked. There had only been one conclusion to draw: what Amelia was going through wasn't physical. It was mental. It was all in her head.

Then Jill did that thing Amelia had seen every single therapist on television do. She pushed a box of tissues toward her client. Toward Amelia. For heaven's sake. She wasn't even crying yet. Or was she? The tiniest amount of moisture had pooled in the corner of her eye. Amelia guessed Jill could read the signs like no other. Pushing the tissues in her direction was her wordless way of saying that Amelia could cry all she wanted. Better here than anywhere else, Amelia thought, and, with a sharp flick of her wrist, pulled a tissue from the box.

"Do you live around here?" Jill's voice was soft.

Amelia nodded. She pressed the tissue to the underside of her nose, just to do something with it. She wasn't ready to admit that she was close to tears. She wasn't one to surrender so easily, which was part of the reason she was sitting in this very chair—she knew that much.

"Have you heard of Glow? The yoga studio down the street from here?"

"I've walked past it." Amelia took a deep breath. Jill was giving her time to regroup.

"Have you considered yoga or meditation?"

"Who hasn't in this day and age?"

Jill just shot her a smile.

"I'm a soccer player," Amelia said. "I'm not the kind of person to fold myself into various impossible positions in the company of a bunch of housewives on mats. It doesn't align with how I think of myself."

"Everything's a scientific analysis with you, isn't it?" Did something in Jill's blue eyes sparkle? Amelia noticed for the first time the darker color of Jill's eyebrows didn't match her blonde hair.

"I'm a soccer player and a scientist." Amelia raised a shoulder.

"What else are you?" Jill quipped—at least it felt like a quip. "What other nouns apply to you?"

Amelia couldn't immediately think of anything else. Sure, she was a lesbian, but she hardly felt like one these days. She hadn't practiced the art of lesbianism in a good long while. She simply hadn't had the energy, despite a new girl on the team showing unmistakable interest in her.

"You're someone's daughter, perhaps?" Jill tried.

"That I am, but my parents live on the Gold Coast and we're not really that close. It's mostly a proximity thing."

"A sibling?"

"That, too, but my only brother lives in London."

"A friend?"

Amelia nodded. "Although a lousy one these past few months."

"Doesn't matter. I'm sure your friends have had their own ups and downs over the years you've known them."

Amelia nodded. What other nouns could she attribute to herself? Her mind was drawing a huge blank. That was what she mainly was these days: someone who drew blanks when asked a direct question. As though her brain was just so tired. As if, after all these years, it had finally had its fill of science, when it had only got energized by it before. The sight of an equation used to light Amelia up like a Christmas tree. Now it made her queasy.

"Do you like to read? Watch TV? Go to the theater? Dine out? Go to the movies?"

"I used to read all the time, but ever since my first panic attack, I can't seem to focus on the words long enough. It's as if the sentences are swimming in front of my eyes."

Jill wrote something down again.

"I do like some fine dining," Amelia admitted. "I'm a restaurant snob, in case you'd like to write that down."

"Do you like art?" Jill asked, seemingly suppressing a grin.

"Good question. I don't really know. There's been a real boom of art galleries in the area the past few years and sometimes I walk past a window and I really like a painting or a sculpture, but I can never really explain why I like it or why it might be good, which really bugs me."

"Does everything need to be explicable?" Jill tilted her head sideways.

"Well, yes." *Duh.*

"Yet not everything is."

"I tend to stay away from inexplicable events or experiences."

"Okay." With a neutral expression on her face, Jill made a note.

Amelia wished she could get a look at that notepad, but she knew that was not how it worked.

"For the record," Amelia said. "As a scientist, I'm hyper-aware of the many events that science can't yet explain. As a biochemical researcher, I know very well that how our brain works is still very much a mystery. But that doesn't mean that there isn't an explanation. It only means we need more time to explain it."

"Have you ever wanted to be anything else other than a scientist?"

"No."

"But would you now say that you've fallen out of love with the sciences somewhat?"

"No." Amelia shook her head vehemently. "My problem

is not with science. It's with what the company I work for, and all the other pharma companies, use science for. As though all it takes is to invent a pill for every ailment. Or worse, an ailment for every medicine we can invent. I've grown so disillusioned by the whole thing. By the financial side of it all." She sighed again. "Maybe by capitalism in general. By the whole notion that money, and nothing else, makes the world go round."

"There's a lot to unpack there." Jill rested her calm gaze on Amelia.

Don't I know it. At least paying someone to listen to all the issues Amelia had acquired over the past forty-five years had the potential of being money well spent. At least Big Pharma had paid her well, and she might as well use the money for something to make her feel better—to counterbalance what earning that money had taken out of her.

Chapter Three

After seeing her new client off, Jill had some free time—something she always scheduled after an appointment with someone new, so she could take the time to process what had been said and go over her notes. After meeting Amelia, Jill needed the break more than anticipated. Perhaps this was due to not having welcomed someone new to her practice in a while, but Jill had more self-awareness than that. She wasn't in the business of fooling herself—that would make her the most hypocritical therapist in all of Sydney. She was attracted to Amelia. It was as simple as that.

Needing to get out of her office, she took her notepad and laptop, and headed to the coffee shop next door. Jill and Patrick had only been in their new office for six months, but already Jill had spent a small fortune on Pink Bean coffee. The Nespresso machine they had in the small kitchen of their practice no longer held any appeal to her. She only used it—and only very reluctantly so—when she needed a quick pick-me-up before an evening appointment, after the Pink Bean had closed.

Kristin, the owner of the Pink Bean, was behind the counter. She greeted Jill as though they'd known each other for years instead of months.

"Small macchiato, coming right up," Kristin said without Jill having to place her order.

"And I'll have some of that banana loaf," Jill said.

"Rough day?" Kristin asked.

"Rough is not the correct word for it." Jill suppressed a smile. "But definitely interesting."

"Sheryl and I had a conversation about you last night," Kristin said, while putting a slice of banana loaf on a small plate. "Say we wanted to go into therapy, would it be ethical for you to take us on as your clients?"

"You mean couples' therapy?" Jill eyed the banana loaf. She broke off a corner and started nibbling. Maybe she should discuss her emotional stress-eating when she next saw her own therapist.

"No, or well, yes, I guess it could be that. But we couldn't agree on whether it would be right for you to see us as clients in your practice. Because you come to the Pink Bean all the time."

"I would probably refer you to my colleague Patrick. That's the beauty of having a joint practice."

"I'm not sure Sheryl would want her therapist to be a man," Kristin said matter-of-factly.

Jill had met Sheryl and she could definitely see that being the case.

"I'm sorry, but is this a hypothetical question or is this for real?"

Kristin handed her a small cup of coffee with a tiny white stain of milk floating at the top. "Purely hypothetical. You've met my other half. You know she's rather fond of a lively debate." Kristin sent Jill a crooked smile.

"Some people are very attached to their opinions," Jill said.

"And some of us have to live with them." Kristin winked at her. "Enjoy. See you later, yeah." She looked over Jill's shoulder at the customer who had just come in.

Jill made her way to a well-lit table by the window. She had quickly become a regular at the Pink Bean, and she wasn't the only one. The woman who ran the yoga studio she had recommended to Amelia—Jill couldn't remember her name—was sitting a few tables down from her, staring intently into a glass of water.

And just like that, Jill's mind was back on Amelia. It had happened before that Jill had felt some kind of attraction to a client. She wasn't made of steel. The difference, this time, she thought, was that it had been instant. As though, the moment Amelia had sat down in front of her, Jill had known she was in trouble. The other quite important distinction was that Jill was single now.

She took another bite of banana loaf. She had tried to convince Kristin to share whatever secret ingredient she used, but to no avail. It was so bloody good.

Jill turned her attention to her notes. Amelia really needed help. And Jill would extend it to her. It was her job—her duty. She was a professional. And health professionals should never get involved with a patient. Ever. That would have to be the end of it.

She started transferring some of her notes to Amelia's client file on her laptop, but she was quickly distracted again by the mention of the Darlinghurst women's soccer team. Jill googled it. There was Amelia in a team photo, towering over the rest of her team, also standing out in the goalkeeper's different color jersey. Amelia Shaw. Never had a woman looked less like a goalie, Jill thought. Or less like she belonged on a soccer pitch. Or a science lab, for that matter.

Amelia's alluring appearance had reminded her of glamorous French actresses on the red carpet. Of gorgeous, husky-voiced—

"Hard at work?" A voice came from next to her.

Jill looked up. "Hey, Liz. Just catching up on some notes." She quickly closed her laptop.

"You weren't browsing the gallery's website for a new acquisition?" Liz glanced at the empty chair next to Jill's.

"Please, be my guest," Jill said. "All my walls are filled to the brim with your fine works of art already."

"We have a very exciting opening in a few weeks. This woman from Brisbane who paints the most unconventional abstracts I've ever seen."

"I'll be there, as usual." Jill smiled at Liz. They weren't friends exactly, but Jill was a big fan of the Griffith-Porter gallery, which Liz and her partner Jessica ran in Potts Point.

"I've been meaning to ask you this for a while now." Liz's smile was so magnetic. Christ, maybe it wasn't just Amelia that Jill was attracted to. Maybe any woman who smiled at her in a certain way moved something inside her these days. She and Rasmus had decided to part ways more than a year ago. Maybe it was Jill's psyche telling her that perhaps it was time to get back into the dating saddle. "Jess and I are having a small soirée this weekend. We'd both very much like for you to come. We regard you as more than a client."

"A party at the gallery?"

"No, at our house," Liz said.

Jill's eyebrows shot up. Maybe a night out with the possibility of meeting some new people was exactly what she needed. "Okay. Sure. I'd love to come." She drew in a breath. "Oh, wait. Are Hera and Kat coming?"

Liz nodded.

"You already know Hera's my client. She may not appreciate her therapist showing up at a private function."

Liz waved her off. "How many times have you and Hera been at the gallery together?"

"I'd prefer to check with her regardless." Jill didn't expect it to be a problem. The first time Jill had run into Hera at the gallery, Hera had looked like a fish out of water, but all the subsequent times, as her relationship with Kat had deepened and stabilized, she'd seemed increasingly at ease. Hera and Jill had even had a few friendly, non-therapeutic chats. Still, it was Jill's job to always put the client first, so when she met with Hera later this week, she would ask her.

"Sure, but I'll be expecting you, anyway." Liz shot her that smile that must have melted dozens of women's hearts before she met Jessica. Thanks to Hera and her relationship with Kat, Jill knew all about Liz and her former co-worker Kat's previous careers as escorts at The Lesbian Experience. "Is it just you or will there be a plus-one?" Liz asked.

"Just me."

"Perfect." Liz rose. "I need to get back. Jess is expecting me."

"Can I bring anything? On Saturday?" Jill looked up at Liz. She figured she and Amelia might be around the same height. Liz also struck Jill as the kind of person who would join an amateur soccer team. She had that sporty, wholesome look about her. Maybe she could broach the subject on Saturday.

"Just your glorious self." She gave Jill a quick wave and turned to leave. Jill followed her with her gaze. Through the large windows of the Pink Bean, she watched Liz unlock her bicycle, a sleek, stark-white racing-bike, sling her long leg over as if it was all she ever did, and whizz off.

After the first time she'd gone to the gallery, she had been equally honest with herself—awareness is the biggest enactor of change and growth, after all. The fact that it was run by two extremely attractive women, a couple no less, was part of the draw. It was one of the reasons Jill kept returning—that, and those two gorgeous women's taste in art, which seemed to align perfectly with hers. She couldn't wait to discover what their home looked like. If Hera consented. And maybe it would help keep her mind off Amelia so that she could be the therapist Amelia needed next time they met.

Chapter Four

IT HAD BEEN YET another soccer practice Amelia'd had to grind her way through on the strength of her willpower. Or maybe it was just plain stubbornness. She made a mental note to discuss this with her new therapist. She'd been making a lot of mental notes the past few days.

But if Amelia didn't make it to practice, she might as well totally give up and accomplish nothing at all. Her days would be completely empty. She needed something to do, even if her body rebelled. Even if her muscles screamed out for rest.

As she brushed some dirt off her knees, she wondered if she should look into a gentler pastime—something like yoga, as Jill had suggested. Even though Amelia had reacted rather defensively when Jill had proposed it, she wasn't above taking a medical professional's advice. That was one of the reasons Amelia had been so happy to get an appointment with Jill, who had a medical degree. As a scientist herself, Amelia could only believe in a qualified doctor helping her. Someone with extensive knowledge of how the body as well as the mind worked. Which was why she'd gotten a referral from her GP to see a psychiatrist with all the required degrees.

None of those degrees had been framed and displayed in Jill's office to impress her clients. Jill's walls were filled with the kind of conceptual art Amelia's scientific brain had no patience for.

"Penny for your thoughts." Sophia, who had joined the team a few months ago, suddenly stood right in front of Amelia.

"Trust me, you don't want to know." Amelia raked her gaze over Sophia. Everything about her made Amelia's gaydar ping, including the purple highlights in her hair. And not that many straight women joined the team.

"You're very wrong about that." Sophia pinned her gaze on Amelia, her hands on her sides. "Are you coming for drinks?"

"Um." Another topic for debate in Amelia's head. Drinks after practice used to be a given, before the smallest, most mundane tasks had started eating away all her energy.

"Come on." Sophia flashed her a smile. "You'd be doing me a huge favor." This wasn't even covert flirting anymore. This was full-on flirty banter. The kind that could not be ignored.

Despite being flattered, Amelia could not be less interested. Sophia seemed like a nice enough girl, but she was far too young and, more importantly, Amelia simply didn't have the energy for any of this. Making it to practice was already a huge feat. A day with an automatic victory. Going on a date with someone, having to make conversation, being interested in another person—these things were so far removed from Amelia's get-through-the-day to-do list, she couldn't even fathom them.

On the flip side, Amelia didn't want to be rude. Sophia was new to the team, while Amelia was, in many ways, an old-timer. It was an unwritten rule that she had to help make Sophia feel welcome. She'd also need to find a way to let her down gently. She knew just the person to help her with that.

From the corner of her eye, she spotted Dawn, one of the few remaining founding members of the Darlinghurst Darlings.

"Sure. I'll come." Amelia managed a weak smile. A full-wattage smile hadn't been part of Amelia's arsenal for a while. Where would she get the vigor for that? "I'll see you in the pub. I need to talk to Dawn about something first."

"Great." Sophia's face was one big grin. She walked past Amelia, barely leaving any space between their bodies as she did.

When Dawn spotted Amelia, she shot her a wink, and walked over to her. "It's not easy being you, is it?" she said. "You have my deepest sympathies, obviously."

"I don't want to hurt her feelings," Amelia whispered.

"A young hottie like that? She'll bounce right back." Dawn threw her arm around Amelia and, together, they walked to the locker room. "Although, and I say this from a place of deep friendship and love, it might not be the worst thing in the world to have a little adventure. You have all this time on your hands now. You might as well use it to have some fun."

Amelia rolled her eyes. Dawn, who seemed to have fallen headfirst into an early midlife crisis, not avoiding any of the clichés that came with it, would say that. She was always trying to live vicariously through Amelia, because Amelia was single, and Dawn had been with Cindy all her adult life.

Amelia leaned against her friend's shoulder. "I need someone to help me deflect young Sophia's advances tonight. Will you be the excellent friend that you are and come to my rescue?"

"Still not feeling it, eh, mate?"

Amelia shook her head.

"How was the therapy session?" Dawn asked. She was the only person Amelia had told.

"Okay, I guess. I don't really have anything to compare it to."

"Did you click with the therapist?"

Had she and Jill clicked? Amelia hadn't really thought about that. Jill had been easy to talk to. Amelia had opened up more than she had expected to. Jill's intelligent gaze and smart questions had managed to draw something from her. And that was, if nothing else, a start. Maybe even the beginning of finding a way out of this dreadful funk, this heavy, black cloud that hung over everything Amelia did.

"Yeah, I think it will be good for me. I think there might be something there."

"That's great." Dawn gave her shoulder a squeeze. "You won't feel like this forever, Melly."

They entered the locker room. *I sure hope not.* But most days—most hours, most minutes—it sure felt like she would.

"De Bruyne is the best player in the world," Sophia said.

"You would say that, if you only follow the Premier League," Dawn said.

"I kind of have a life," Sophia said. "Pubs to go to. Women to date. You know, that sort of thing."

She did know how to put Dawn in her place. Amelia had to give her that. It even made her snicker a little.

"I have a wife and two small children," Dawn said. "And I think Megan Rapinoe is the best player in the world."

Sophia almost snorted her beer through her nose.

It looked as if Dawn and Sophia would become fast friends. Which was all fine with Amelia, as long as Sophia didn't focus all her attention back on her. Dawn was doing a brilliant job of deflecting it.

"Who's your favorite player?" Sophia turned to Amelia.

"I don't really have one. I mean, I guess it varies." During another sleepless night, Amelia had signed on for a sports channel that showed matches from all the European leagues, all day long. She'd watched so much soccer of late, she was surprised she wasn't sick of it yet. She still had trouble remembering the players' names though. But she had enough personal pride to not just blurt out the first obvious one that came to mind.

Sophia didn't grill her any further. "Can you believe that the French national women's team has zero out players?" She shook her head. "Statistically, it's impossible." She ran a hand through her short, purple-streaked hair. "Also, do they think we're blind and totally devoid of gaydar?"

"Maybe the French are much more uptight than we think they are," Dawn said. "Just because they have a pair of naked boobs in every single movie, doesn't mean they're not a homophobic nation."

"I think it's a soccer issue as well," Amelia cut in. "Not one male footballer in Europe has come out of the closet. Not a single one. How is that possible? It must be a culture thing. And a money thing, for sure." Argh. Money. Maybe Amelia should sell her condo, take her savings, and go live off the land somewhere. Escape the system she had come to loathe so much. Soccer was possibly even worse than Big Pharma, although, as a woman with a heart for science, she knew very well she was comparing apples and oranges.

"I keep a list," Sophia said, "of all the soccer players I presume are gay. It's quite long." She started to count on her fingers. "First, there's—"

"I think it's time I go home to the Mrs." Dawn cut her off. "Sorry, Soph. Melly, do you want a lift?"

Amelia lived walking distance from the pub, but she knew that Dawn was saving her from Sophia's flirting.

"Oh, come on," Sophia pleaded. "One last beverage. On me."

"Cindy will have my head on a spike if I come home smelling like a pub," Dawn said. "And I need to get something from Amelia's first."

Sophia scrunched her face into a disappointed scowl. "Next time."

Both Amelia and Dawn nodded. They said their goodbyes and went on their way.

"Do you want me to come up for a bit?" Dawn asked, when they had reached Amelia's building. "For a chat?"

Amelia shook her head. "Thanks for asking, but I'm beat. Go home to your wife and kiss the kids for me."

"Okay." Dawn leaned in and pecked Amelia on the cheek. "See you at the game on Saturday. Cindy's bringing the kids."

Julian, Dawn and Cindy's oldest, was Amelia's godson. She hadn't been much of a godmother of late. Thank goodness he wanted to be a goalkeeper at the moment—much to Dawn's, who was a striker, dismay. At least Amelia could give him some easy tips on goalkeeping.

She dragged herself up the stairs, took a shower, and flicked on the soccer channel.

Chapter Five

JILL HAD BEEN single for almost a year. She was used to going places on her own. What she wasn't necessarily used to was going somewhere that might very well be packed with women who liked women. Jill happened to like women, too. As well as men. Because she'd been with Rasmus for so long, most people who only knew her superficially usually assumed she was straight. She used to make a point of correcting them, but still, in many ways there was no such thing as being openly bisexual. And she hadn't done any correcting in a while.

A bottle of nice Champagne in hand, she rang the bell of what looked like a very posh house in Potts Point. She knew all about Jessica Porter's pedigree. Behind that door, she expected to see nothing but opulence—and lesbians.

Liz ushered her in. The first guest Jill recognized was Kristin. It was good to see a familiar face. *Wait.* Was that Caitlin James sitting between Kristin and Sheryl?

"Hey." Jill hadn't seen Hera walk up to her. She must have come from behind. "Don't worry, Jill," Hera's voice was light, her tone naughty. "Everyone here knows you're my shrink. This shouldn't be awkward *at all*." She slanted toward Jill, who had to take a split second to parse what was happening. Then they exchanged a quick kiss on the cheek. "Shall I introduce you?"

Just then, Josephine Greenwood walked out of the kitchen, carrying a tray of cheese. Jill felt that both Liz and Hera'd had ample opportunity to warn her that tonight would be celebrity-studded. Although perhaps, to them, Caitlin and Jo were just friends.

Hera introduced Jill to Caitlin and Jo. Jill already knew Jessica, Sheryl and Kristin. Then the bell rang and two more women arrived. Jill recognized the ginger-haired woman who ran Glow. Her partner was introduced to Jill as Martha, who was also a colleague of Sheryl's at the university. Then Jill found herself surrounded by no less than five lesbian couples. Her mind was so busy trying to catch up, she hadn't even noticed the art on the walls.

It took about half an hour for Jill to convince herself that this wasn't all part of a set-up. That a twelfth guest wouldn't soon arrive—a single woman like Jill. But no one else turned up. Which wasn't that much of a surprise because Jill hadn't spoken to any of these people about her sexuality. Or maybe lesbians made a similar but opposite assumption to heterosexuals. Maybe they presumed women were gay until proven otherwise. Jill shook the thought off as silly and tried to tune back into the conversation.

Still, it was difficult not to wonder why she was here tonight. Because of that, it was equally difficult not to feel a little out of place. And she was also a touch disappointed there weren't any other single women present. But at least her mind was kept too busy to linger on Amelia.

She glanced at Hera, whose hand rested in Kat's lap. Jill had witnessed Hera's transformation from a grieving woman who clung to solitude as though it was a life raft, to this brand-new person who sparkled with vitality and enjoyed the company of others. Meeting Kat certainly had played a part in that. But Jill was proud of her own contribution—of the work she had done with Hera. There hadn't been a quick fix—there never was. But look at her now. Hera was thriving.

"Have you taken Jill for a tour?" Jessica asked Liz.

"I've been a touch busy waiting on you, darling." Liz shot Jessica a smile. "Jess has officially been in remission from breast cancer for two years." She held up her Champagne flute. "So I told her I'd take care of everything tonight."

"Nothing new there," Caitlin said. "I'm sure you've noticed by now, Liz, but Jessica's quite used to everything being taken care of for her."

"You're one to talk," Josephine said.

"Darling, I'm a very busy woman." She cast Josephine a loving glance.

"Caitlin only has a few more screen-worthy years left in her," Sheryl said to Josephine. "It's best to let her be busy and spoiled just a little while longer, before she has to shuffle off into anonymity."

"Here's to Jess." Caitlin ignored everyone's jibes and lifted her glass. "The best boss I've ever had. You're sorely missed at the network."

They all toasted to Jessica's health, then Liz rose and invited Jill to follow her. She escorted her into the hallway and stopped in front of a painting Jill easily recognized as by Alyssa Myles, whose work she had seen on display at the gallery.

"It's so wonderful," Jill said. "That Jessica's better now."

"She's not totally out of the woods, but yeah, it's great news. Whenever she goes for a checkup, it's so nerve-racking.

We have a party afterward every time. Either to celebrate, which has been the case so far—" She rapped her knuckles against a sideboard that was home to about a dozen picture frames. "Knock on wood. Or, if the worst-case scenario ever came to pass, then to commiserate with our friends."

Friends. Liz hit the nail right on the head. Jill was merely an acquaintance to these women. She didn't even know Jessica had battled cancer.

"Can I ask you something?" Jill turned her body fully to Liz.

"Of course." Liz took a sip from her glass.

"Clearly, you're all quite close. I'm very grateful for the invitation, but ever since I arrived, I've been trying to figure out why I'm here."

"Oh, I hope you're not feeling like a fifth—or should I say eleventh wheel. That was never my intention. It was a spur-of-the-moment thing when I ran into you the other day, but only because Jess and I are very interested in getting to know you better and, well…" She narrowed her eyes. "Kat and I also have a bet to settle when it comes to you."

"You do?" Jill was confused.

"Every few weeks, you come hang out with a bunch of lesbians at the gallery. Then, you suddenly started turning up at the Pink Bean, which isn't a lesbian venue as such, but it is very gay. It made my gaydar ping. Jess says I'm reading too much into it. We've asked Hera, but she doesn't know anything about your personal life."

"Seriously?" Jill didn't know whether to be flattered to have caught Liz's attention or offended by her juvenile interest in her love life. "That's why I'm here?"

"No—I mean, that's not the main reason, of course." The thing with Liz was that she could say anything in a way that would make you accept and, if necessary, forgive her on the spot. The woman oozed charisma—she was born to seduce. "Jess and I like you, Jill. You've supported us from the start. That means a great deal to us. Honestly." She painted on that huge smile of hers. "But yes, I won't lie—it's not my style. I'm curious about you. Which doesn't mean you have to tell us anything about yourself, of course." She tilted her head. "I pride myself on how well I can read a person in a certain situation. I can probably figure it out for myself after tonight."

If Liz hadn't just toasted to her partner's health, Jill could have easily mistaken this conversation for flirting.

"At least you weren't taking pity on me," Jill said.

"How so?" Liz sounded genuine enough.

"When I saw it was all couples plus me, for a minute, I thought you were setting me up on some sort of convoluted blind date."

"Oh." Liz's eyebrows shot up. "I hadn't really thought about that, to be honest, which doesn't mean I can't make something happen for you." She waggled her eyebrows suggestively. "I have a lot of… connections."

"Please don't corrupt my therapist." For a woman with such a stocky build, Hera had sure mastered the art of sneaking up on people. "Not that I would think less of you, Jill." Hera shot her a crooked smile.

"You shouldn't think anything of me at all," Jill blurted out. "I mean, my personal life shouldn't be of concern to any of my clients. Therapy's all about *you*." Jill could only conclude it was she who was nervous being around Hera in this particular situation. It was all well and good at a busy gallery with dozens of people milling around and chattering away. Tonight's gathering was much more intimate, and it threw Jill a bit.

"Of course, your clients will wonder about you. That's only natural." Hera sounded a touch offended.

"It is, to a certain extent."

"Maybe I should leave you ladies to it," Liz said. "Sounds to me like you have some urgent therapist-client stuff to duke out. We'll resume the tour later." Liz regarded her intently for a moment—as though she was taking the measure of Jill. The night had most certainly taken a turn for the uncomfortable. Liz disappeared into the living room.

"Typical Liz," Hera said. "Start something, then walk away."

"Is it?" Jill catalogued it as a trait she should pay attention to in the future.

"Can we sit for a minute?" Hera pointed at two overstuffed armchairs lining the wall.

Jill wasn't prepared for an impromptu therapy session, although she'd been working with Hera for so long, she didn't need any preparation.

"I think the time has come for me to stop seeing you as my therapist. It just occurred to me, as we were all sitting together, that I would rather have you as my friend than my therapist. If that is at all possible. If it's not a conflict of interest."

Jill wasn't expecting that. She took a drink so she could gather her thoughts. "I'm not in the habit of befriending former clients. It makes the relationship very lopsided. I know an awful lot about you, Hera. Every detail of which will remain confidential forever. But it doesn't really make for an even starting point for any kind of relationship." An image of Amelia slipped into Jill's mind.

"But I like that you know these things about me. Even though you've always clearly stated that you and I aren't friends, there have been times that I considered you my only friend in the world. Most certainly my only confidante. You have done so much for me, Jill. I may not know a whole lot about you, but I know instinctively that you are a good person with a big heart. That's all I need to know, really."

"Wow." Jill couldn't help but break into a wide smile. "Thanks, Hera."

"I was such a mess when I first came to see you."

Jill nodded, which made her feel like she was in session again.

"You weren't the first psychiatrist I tried, but after our first session, I sort of knew you'd be the last. And I was right." Hera grinned at her. Kat had managed to posh her up a touch, but she still clearly favored T-shirts over blouses, albeit less worn ones. "And let me tell you something in confidence." She pointed her thumb at the living room door. "I might call that lot in there my friends these days, but they can still intimidate the hell out of me."

"You seem pretty comfortable with them."

"I am, but…" She cast a glance about the opposite wall. "I still don't know the first thing about art and I'd honestly much rather watch the footy than *The Caitlin James Show*." Hera chuckled. "I've had Jo's album on repeat though. On a job, it's really great for singing along to."

"It's wonderful to see you so happy, Hera."

"It's wonderful to feel this way. To be here. To have all this friendship and love in my life after Sam died. Remember when I came to you with all my doubts about Kat? Turns out taking that job at my nephew's coffee shop was the best thing that ever happened to me."

Warmth bloomed in Jill's chest. "How's Rocco?"

"Camp as ever." She spread her fingers over her biceps. "Muscles this big." She grinned. "But he's doing absolutely fine." She pursed her lips. "How about you come down to the Bondi Pink Bean one of these days? I'll treat you to a fancy coffee. I even know how to make them these days."

"I'd love to."

"Phew." Hera pretended to wipe sweat from her brow.

"Knowing me so well, I was worried you'd be completely put off by the thought of being friends with me."

"I'm here tonight, aren't I?"

"Sure, but I'm under no illusion you're here for me, Doc." Hera slanted her torso closer to Jill. "Don't tell me Liz and Jess are celebrating Jess's remission anniversary by, um, *opening up*?"

"What do you mean?" Jill wasn't quite following.

"Be warned, Doc. You hang out with this bunch for long enough and you will not believe some of the things you'll find out."

"Tell me." If Hera was no longer going to be her client, Jill might as well find out some of the origins of the stories the other women had alluded to over the course of the evening.

Hera chuckled heartily. "It's not my place, but you're bound to find out soon enough." That was Hera all right—never one to dish another person's secrets. "How about we go back in before anyone gets any ideas in their head?" She winked. "About me needing an emergency therapy session tonight."

Jill followed Hera back into the living room. She'd been right after all. Despite the lack of other singles, tonight might be just the thing to keep her mind off Amelia.

Chapter Six

"I'M SO SORRY." Amelia couldn't believe she'd forgotten to switch off her phone. The Darlinghurst Darlings' WhatsApp group was always buzzing with gifs and inside jokes—hardly ever with any actual soccer-related messages.

"It's okay. Clients forget all the time," Jill said.

As she switched her phone to silent, Amelia noticed that the latest message was a private one from Sophia. It wasn't the first one Amelia had received. She heaved a sigh. "There's this woman on the team. She's coming on a bit strong. It's been bugging me."

"Is she flirting with you?"

"Any chance she gets."

"That must be flattering."

Amelia frowned. "Sure. I mean, she's perfectly lovely, but…" Oh. Had she just inadvertently come out to her therapist? She'd probably done so already when she'd told Jill about the soccer team. But still. This warranted closer scrutiny of Jill's face. Not that Amelia expected a hyper-educated psychiatrist to have a problem with that. "I'm sorry I didn't mention it during our previous session. I'm gay. I just… I don't know. I guess I was waiting to see how our first session went and then it didn't really come up again."

"That's perfectly fine. You can't tell me everything about yourself in one session." Jill's smile remained as friendly and warm as before.

"It's not very relevant to what I'm going through, so…"

"Tell me about this woman who texted you… Do you like her?"

Amelia could only assume Jill had a good therapeutic reason to inquire further. "Her name's Sophia. She's an excellent soccer player. Midfield. Great on possession. A real asset to the team."

Jill nodded, a benign smile on her face. Oh, right. She probably wasn't asking about Sophia's position on the pitch. "She's in her twenties. Late twenties, but still. Either way, I'm just not up to dating anyone right now. If anything, I feel like I should date myself, you know? Work on the self-love and self-care and all that."

"Of course. Tell me about your week."

"We lost our game on Saturday. I let in two goals. One of which could have been easily avoided—" Amelia caught Jill's glance.

"You sure do love soccer."

"I'm sorry. It's kind of all I have going on at the moment. Taking a loss is extra hard these days. Even though our league is just for fun. There's no relegation or promotion. Just the same old six teams playing against each other every week, year in, year out."

"You can talk about soccer all you want, but never assume I know all that much about it." Jill held up her hand. "That doesn't mean I'm not interested, however."

"I'm not coming here to talk about soccer, though, am I?" Amelia tried a grin.

Jill ran a hand through her hair. She was definitely attractive. Maybe it was her warmth that made Amelia think that, as she barely noticed women in that way these days.

"So, soccer was lousy and you have no interest in dating." Jill pursed her lips while she made a quick note. "Did anything else happen this week? How did you feel after our first session?"

"Um…" Amelia paused while she thought. "Maybe… as though there's hope for me yet."

Jill didn't respond. A silence fell.

"I mean, um, I felt relieved that I had come and that the first session was over." Amelia considered what Dawn had asked her after practice the other day, about she and her therapist 'clicking'. She had given it some thought and had concluded that she and Jill were a match. She smiled ruefully at her choice of word. "I guess I was also relieved that we seem to get along. From what I've heard from other people, it's not always a given."

"Correct. Not everyone would feel comfortable with me as their therapist."

"Do *you* ever not feel comfortable with a client?" Amelia couldn't help but ask. She was interested in that sort of stuff—in what happened behind the scenes.

"It has happened, but this is my job. Part of that is getting past any uncomfortable feelings."

"One of the reasons it took me so long to take this step—to seek professional help for my mental health—is that therapy is something very hard for me to get my head around. Take any screening for a personality disorder, for instance. There's so much subjectivity at play. As in that it matters who is doing the evaluation. It can never be entirely objective because of the human factor, and therefore never truly scientific, unless there are actual brain scans involved."

"And yet I consider my job to be very scientific. So much research has been done. I could spend every single weekend reading up on the latest studies in the field and I would still only get through a fraction of them."

"I don't doubt that for a second, but it's not the same as putting a cell under a microscope to study. It's not a hard science."

"You're right. It's not exactly the same, but it doesn't have to be the same to be effective—or true."

"I'm sorry. I was getting on my high horse again. I do that sometimes."

"I'm not that easy to offend, Amelia. In fact, I welcome your view. I like to be challenged. But… maybe we should get back to you now. Back to how you've been feeling. Earlier, you mentioned 'dating yourself'. It's a concept I like very much. Have you been able to do anything this week that would count as going on a date with yourself?"

"Being single, every time I go out to eat alone is like going on a date with myself."

"Is that something you do often? Go out by yourself?"

"I used to, but I tend to stay in more these days. Until I find the walls are closing in and then I need to get out. My best friend Dawn and her wife have been great. They drag me out of the house at least once a week. I'm godmother to their eldest. Too many times, however, I've been absolute shit company to them. It's like…" Amelia didn't have to try hard to recall the feeling, but it was hard to put into words. "Something's been taken from me in here." She put her hand on her chest. "That spark. Whatever it is that makes you get up in the morning and look forward to the day. It's gone and I don't know how to get it back."

Jill uncrossed and recrossed her legs. "That's your body telling you that you've pushed it too far, that it can only take so much."

"I've been off work for weeks now and I still feel the same."

"I'm not going to lie to you, Amelia. This will take time. It took years and years for your body to give out. For that panic attack to build and then to recur. Something like that can't be undone in a few weeks." Jill paused. "But it's not only that you pushed yourself too hard at work. It's more complex than that. Human beings always are." She painted on a small smile. "On top of not giving yourself enough time to recharge your batteries, and completely draining them, you also started to question the meaning of your work. I'd like to address that, if you think you're up for it."

"I kind of fell out of love with the job. It's not my job or my industry that has changed. It's me."

"What do you think brought about that change?"

"I don't know. It happened over time. Little things, I guess. Things that added up to an utter disdain for the 'pill industry', which is what I sometimes call it now. The times we live in as well, of course. Because times do change." Amelia paused to take a breath. "You have to understand that I've always believed that the medicine we developed would fundamentally help people. And it's not as though I was this naive young thing when I started. I already knew money was the biggest motivator of companies. But maybe my view on money and how it affects people and the world at large, has changed."

"How does it affect people?"

"That's another thing that's been niggling at me..." Looking around Jill's office, taking in her furniture and all the art on the walls, Amelia guessed that Jill enjoyed many of the same privileges that she did. "Who am I to disparage money? Is it even my place to get depressed about the role it plays in our life? I have plenty, while there are so many people who have to scrape to get by. But that is part of the problem, of course. I can get so lost in these infinite tangents. It starts with a simple enough premise: Big Pharma is all about big profit. But once you really start to think about it, it's not as simple as that. It's complex. And I try and try to uncomplicate it, because that's what I do."

Amelia paused to catch her breath.

"But it goes on and on. The thing is that I used to enjoy a good old discussion about money and inequality and all the things that go wrong in this world—because don't they all start with money? But lately, it just makes me feel utterly discouraged. Empty. Asking myself what the point of it all even is?"

"For the record," Jill said, "just now, you didn't sound discouraged at all. You very much sounded as though you care a great deal."

"But what does it matter if I care?"

"Maybe it doesn't matter to you right now, but it matters in the grand scheme of things."

Amelia shook her head. Maybe Jill didn't exactly get what she was trying to say. Even having this conversation was tiring. Another extended silence descended. Amelia was too exhausted to fill it.

"Have you considered a change of career?" Jill asked after a while.

"Of course. In the end, it might be the only solution."

"Which direction are you thinking about heading into?"

"Women's soccer manager," Amelia joked, because she really needed some lightness right now.

Jill didn't seem to get the joke. Her facial expression remained the same. "Maybe it's too early to think about a new professional direction, but… whenever you mention the word *soccer*, your eyes light up. Maybe you should set yourself a little project as a hobby. Try to get your 40+ league off the ground. Or something else, as long as it's soccer-related. Take it from there."

"Maybe." Amelia assumed her 40+ league would never

happen because it was nothing more than a pipe dream. Something she liked to cling to because she simply didn't have that much else going on in her life. "Maybe I should start with a team instead of a league. Maybe I can find a way to make the team good enough to compete in the current league."

"There you go," Jill said. "Run with it. Take the challenge. What have you got to lose?" Jill sounded more enthused now than Amelia.

She would give it some serious thought, however. She didn't have anything else to fill her days with.

Chapter Seven

AFTER JILL HAD SHOWN Amelia out, she stood with her back against the door for long minutes, as though rooted to the spot. What she had wanted to say to her new client was, "Look in the mirror. Look at that splendid, igniting smile when it comes through, and soak up all its energy. Look into your beautiful, brown eyes and let their soulfulness fill you with—" She had to stop herself. She shouldn't even have been thinking those thoughts while in session. What was she? Newly graduated and not in control of her impulses? But decades of experience didn't inoculate you against the mind-altering effect a gorgeous woman could have on you. That much was clear. And that voice. Jill wanted to bathe in it—drown in it. At the very least, she'd like to lie next to Amelia—preferably naked—and hide in the deep, soothing comfort of it while she told her a story, any story.

What Jill really should do was go to her colleague, Patrick, and confess to him what kind of a foolish woman she was being, harboring thoughts unworthy of her profession. Patrick would understand. He might be able to take on Amelia as his own client, although Jill wasn't sure that was advisable. In any case, there was only one person's interest she should focus on: Amelia's.

But Amelia had just told her that she was glad she'd found Jill. And it wasn't as if, were she to drop Amelia as a client, it would magically become ethical for Jill to date her. First of all, Amelia was in no state to date anyone. She was putting herself and her life back together after a severe case of burnout. Jill knew better than anyone that recovery from burnout was a delicate process not to be tinkered with. There was no winning play here.

Instead of waiting for Patrick to finish his session, she took a deep breath, and tried to banish the thought of Amelia from her mind. *Good luck with that.* Thank goodness she was seeing her own therapist tomorrow. Vic would set her straight.

Victoria Longe was years past the government's official retirement date. "The day I retire," she always claimed, "is the day they put me in a coffin." Old age hadn't made Vic any less feisty. But she'd always been compassionate and understanding, offering Jill a different perspective when she needed it. She sorely needed it today.

The more she tried not to think of Amelia, the more she did. That was psychology 101, of course. It didn't help that Jill knew this better than anyone. What she had told herself, however, to the point that she was more than ready to believe it, was that her experience with Amelia had been a pretty straightforward case of what the French called *coup de foudre*. She'd been struck by the lightning of lust. In life, it was a simple case of acknowledging that these things happened. The trouble only occurred when you started to attach meaning or, heaven forbid, importance to such an event.

While a strike of lightning could not be undone, it could be managed. Jill could not be un-struck, but she could use her intellect to deal with this. Her dignity. Her will to truly help Amelia. And she had Vic.

"What makes this woman so special?" Vic asked after Jill had explained the situation. "Apart from her being so—and I quote—'devastatingly gorgeous'?"

"I don't know—yet. Isn't that usually the case with lust at first sight?"

Vic gave her an admonishing look. And sure, Jill should know better. But in this room, opposite Vic, she didn't want to be a psychiatrist. She was just a woman who needed some help.

"Okay. Fine." Under Vic's withering stare, Jill always acquiesced quickly. "She's vulnerable right now, yet it's as though I can see right past it and I can see her inner strength. The strength she thinks she has lost; I can almost smell it. It's just waiting, biding its time. I so desperately want to help her find it again."

"I'm not going to mince my words here," Vic said. "You're projecting. It's a classic case of countertransference."

"No." Did Vic really think Jill hadn't thought of that herself? "It's not that. Maybe it's just purely physical. Maybe she's just really my type, you know."

"Wasn't Rasmus a blue-eyed, blond-haired Swede?" Vic asked.

"Rasmus is also a man. My taste in women is very different."

"I've known you for a very long time, Jill, and that's the first I've ever heard you talk of having a particular taste in people. Or that you might even have a type."

"Maybe it's not her, then. Maybe it's me. Maybe it's my subconscious telling me it's about time I put myself out there again."

"Now we're getting somewhere." Vic swept her long, gray braid off her shoulders. "I'm glad you can still be honest, even when under the influence of carnal desires."

"I met a bunch of women over the weekend. A very interesting lot." Jill told Vic about her evening at Liz and Jess's house and ended with Hera's request to become friends rather than client and therapist.

"I'm old-school," Vic said. "I don't think that's appropriate."

"You've never built a friendship with a former client?"

"Of course not. Clients are not friends. You know this, Jill. We have a code."

"But life doesn't always go in a way that allows us to stick to all the codes."

"Even though it's exactly in those times that a code can be a much-needed moral compass."

Sometimes, a session with Vic resembled a conversation with her conscience. "Now that our practice has moved, I run into these women at the coffee shop next door all the time. Are you saying it's unethical for me to get to know them because they're friends with a former client of mine? It's a small world. I've been doing this job for a long time and I've seen hundreds of people."

"I don't think this is about Hera at all," Vic said. "I think this is about you having to decide, sooner rather than later, whether to keep Amelia as a client or not."

"What do you think I should do?" Jill asked.

"You could refer her to a colleague that you know well and trust. Someone you know will give her the best care."

"I could or I should?"

"You *should*. You're not the only therapist in Sydney who can help her. Off the top of my head, at least four others come to mind."

"They would need to be a medical doctor. A psychiatrist, like me. Otherwise, she won't be able to trust the process."

"All due respect, but that's bullshit."

"To her, it's not. You know how important the first few sessions are. To establish that rapport, the initial seed of trust. This woman, she's all about the hard sciences. If she has to start over with someone new, someone who isn't a doctor, I fear she might give up before she starts to benefit from it."

"We both know that in the short term, at least, an appointment with a psychiatrist is very hard to come by. She was lucky to have got one with you in the first place."

Jill had to check herself. Was she being totally honest? Or was she twisting Amelia's words to fit her own narrative—to find the ultimate excuse to keep her on. "I could call in a favor from a friend." Jill had done similar favors for colleagues in the past.

"Sounds to me as though you know very well what you should do, Jill." Vic rested her olive-green gaze on her.

"Oh, I know." She all but threw her hands up in desperation. "I know I'm bargaining with myself and I know how pathetic it makes me look."

"Maybe you should go on a date," Vic said. "Not with your client, of course."

"At my age, the whole dating thing is quite daunting. Rasmus and I were together for such a long time. I don't even know where to start."

"I wish I could give you some practical advice, but I'm afraid I would only be repeating whatever it is you'd find in a women's magazine."

"Maybe I should hang out at the Pink Bean more. Spread the word that I'm single and looking. Surely, I can't be the only person on the pull."

"That would actually be an excellent strategy. Let all

your friends and acquaintances know that you're open to meeting someone new. Friends of friends are always a good starting point."

Jill wondered how on earth she'd keep her mind off Amelia, if she ever did find someone suitable to go on a date with. But she had to. She had a lightning strike to manage. First, however, she would need to tell Amelia that she had to refer her to a colleague, and why. Before she did that, she needed to find someone to refer her to. It all sounded so difficult, like such a bloody kerfuffle that she didn't want to deal with. Of course not. All she wanted was to keep seeing Amelia.

At the end of her session with Vic, Jill stood and offered Vic a brief smile.

"I hope you have some good news for me next time. On all fronts," Vic said.

Jill hoped so too.

Chapter Eight

AMELIA HAD TAKEN A SHOWER, washed her hair, put on clean clothes, and had gathered the last scraps of energy she could muster to go out for a coffee down the street, only to find her regular coffee shop closed. There was no explanation posted on the door as to why, nor a reopening date. Amelia hoped it was just for today.

Since she was out and about, she decided to go for a stroll. It was a lovely late-spring day. And she needed coffee. Every coffee shop she passed—and there were quite a few in her neighborhood—she debated whether to stop and go in, but she didn't. To her surprise, she was enjoying her walk. The fresh air. The sight of other people. The buzz of Sydney. It didn't appall her the way it had last time she had ventured out for errands. Maybe because today she had no errands to run. She was simply out for the sake of it. While it had been hard to get herself out the door, now that she was, she enjoyed the light breeze wafting through her hair. She smiled at the dogs out on a walk with their owners and silently acquiesced to her inner voice saying she should really get a dog of her own.

Amelia had walked quite a few blocks, meandering this way and that, when she realized she was on the street of Jill's office. She hadn't taken the direct route she used when going to an appointment. Yet, this was where she had ended up. Was it some subconscious thing? Because those two sessions with Jill had given her a glimmer of hope and a tiny boost of energy? Maybe starting therapy was the very reason she was even able to leave her house this afternoon. Jill should know a thing or two about the subconscious. Amelia made a mental note to ask her next time she saw her, which was in three days.

When she'd come to her appointments, Amelia had noticed the coffee shop next to Jill's office. She might as well go for a coffee there. She walked in and queued. There were two people in front of her. She spotted the sign above the counter. *The Pink Bean.* What an odd name. Then she noticed the rainbow sticker just below the counter. Ah, it was an LGBTQ+ thing. That made more sense. She checked out the girl behind the counter. *Hm, maybe.* Amelia's gaydar hadn't had a lot of practice lately. Except with Sophia. But that wasn't even a matter of gaydar, what with the unmistakable way she was coming on to Amelia.

When it was her turn, Amelia ordered a cappuccino. She eyed the barista while she prepared the beverage. Either way, she was too young for Amelia's 40+ soccer league. But, if she did run with the idea, as Jill had advised her to, this coffee shop could be a good place to recruit.

Amelia found a table in the front. The weather was warm enough for all the windows to be open. She glanced backward to check out the clientele. A few young mothers with prams. A twenty-something guy with a man-bun working on his laptop. Two middle-aged women deep in conversation. Somehow, they didn't look like they would be into soccer. Then again, Amelia had heard that said about herself so many times, and she was *so* into soccer, sometimes, it was hard to find her way out. To think of something else for a change.

She sipped from her cappuccino. The coffee was damn good here. She would remember that. Maybe, before her next therapy session, she should come early and have one. It might give her some more energy to tackle therapy with. She couldn't help but wonder what her therapist thought of her. But surely, in her line of work, Jill met all sorts of people in different kinds of conditions. If anything, in her therapist's office was exactly where Amelia could just let it all out. She didn't have to pretend to be full of life in front of Jill. That was the whole point.

From the corner of her eye, she saw someone walk into the shop. Even though Amelia didn't get a good look, the figure seemed familiar. Speak of the devil. It was Jill.

Amelia felt like she was spying on her as Jill headed to the counter and placed her order. Should she say something? What was the protocol in these circumstances? Jill chatted with the barista as if she knew her pretty well. She probably came here all the time.

One of the middle-aged women called to Jill and asked her to join them at their table. Jill waved them off and pointed at her laptop. Then, her gaze must have landed on Amelia. Something in her eyes changed. A sort of stunned look came over her—as though it was highly improbable that she would ever run into a client in this particular coffee shop, despite it being right next door to her office. Only then did Jill's lips curl into a smile. She gave Amelia a nod of recognition. Amelia smiled and nodded back. She would let Jill take the lead on how to handle this situation.

Jill's coffee was ready, and Amelia averted her gaze. It was hard to relax though, now that she knew Jill was somewhere inside the coffee shop.

"Hey." Not somewhere inside, then. She was right behind Amelia.

Amelia glanced up at her. "Hi."

"I didn't want you to feel awkward or anything." Jill followed up with a weird kind of chuckle. "And I wanted to say hello, of course."

"Sure." If it had been anyone else, Amelia would have invited them to join her without even giving it a second thought. But Jill was her therapist. "Hello." She flashed Jill a smile. "How are you?"

"Um, yeah, fine." Was Amelia imagining things or did Jill look flustered? Maybe she was meeting someone. She could be blushing for a million different reasons Amelia knew nothing about. Amelia opened up to Jill but the nature of their relationship precluded any reciprocity. "Um." Jill shifted her weight around. The cup and saucer she held rattled, as though her hands were shaking. "Can I sit with you for a minute, Amelia?"

"Of course." Amelia drew her chair back and made room for Jill to pass. "Be my guest."

Jill glanced around as though she was about to confide a secret in Amelia. If she didn't look exactly like Dr. Jill Becket, Amelia's psychiatrist, the woman she had gone to see twice in the past two weeks, Amelia would have thought the woman sitting across from her was a different person. What was going on here? Why was Jill acting all cagey?

"Are you okay, Jill?"

Jill nodded unconvincingly. "I need to talk to you about something, but, on second thought, I'm not sure this is the right time or place."

Amelia tilted her head. "Is it about my therapy?"

"Never mind." Jill waved her hand about. "We'll talk about it in your next session." She seemed to relax a little.

"How are you?" She locked her gaze on Amelia's for an instant, but looked away again quickly.

"I'm having a pretty good day today, actually."

"That's great." Jill sipped from her tiny espresso cup. "Do you come here often?"

"No. My regular coffee shop is closed and I ended up here somehow." Amelia leaned over the table. In Jill's office, the chairs were set up at a respectable distance. "Is it just my imagination or is this place rather gay?"

"I'm not sure what exactly makes a coffee shop 'gay'," Jill said. She seemed to have possession of all her confidence again. "But the Pink Bean is definitely LGBTQ-friendly."

"It's just the name and the rainbow sticker and... I don't know. The vibe, I guess."

"The owners are lesbians," Jill said. "They often organize evening activities that are quite queer-inspired."

"Right." So Amelia had been correct. Maybe something else had awakened inside her. "You must come here often, what with your office being next door."

"We only moved our practice here six months ago, but yes, since then, my caffeine consumption has reached staggering heights." As though to prove a point, she downed the rest of her coffee.

"It's a lovely place," Amelia said. "The coffee is to die for."

"A million times better than my Nespresso machine next door." Jill smiled a different kind of smile now. It wasn't one of her professional therapy-smiles, at least not one Amelia could remember seeing. "I should leave you to it, Amelia."

"It's fine. If this isn't inappropriate, of course." She glanced at Jill's laptop. "I wouldn't want to keep you from your work." She remembered how Jill had gestured at the two women who had beckoned her to sit with them earlier, indicating she had work to do.

"It's unusual, but on the other hand, it's only normal that I would bump into a client now and then, especially someone who lives locally. How was soccer this weekend?"

"The game was a draw. One nice save from yours truly. I did let one slip through, though." She appreciated Jill asking. Amelia did understand why this was unusual. Jill had information about her that allowed her to ask personal questions, while Amelia knew nothing about Jill. She didn't even know if it was okay to inquire.

"And Sophia?" Jill had painted a proper grin on now.

"She scored, so…" Amelia grinned back.

Jill leaned back. For some reason, she heaved a sigh. "I need to get back to the office, Amelia. Lovely seeing you." And just like that, as though something urgent had just occurred to her, she rose and left.

Chapter Nine

JILL COULD KICK HERSELF. What did she think she was doing? This managing of a bloody lightning strike was proving much more difficult in practice than in theory. Not that it was an excuse, but Amelia had looked so scrumptious. So impossible to resist saying hello to. For a second, Jill had believed this was her chance to tell Amelia that she would need to refer her on. But Amber and the woman who managed her studio, Micky-something, were sitting two tables down from Amelia. And who knew who else might walk in? Sheryl might have turned up at their table and Sheryl had an uncanny gift for rooting out people's intentions. It also wouldn't have been fair to drop Amelia as a client in a coffee shop, when they had run into each other by coincidence only. Other than all of that, Jill had yet to decide upon the reason she should give Amelia. In her heart of hearts, she knew she needed to be honest. She owed Amelia that much, lest she think it was something about her. Technically, it was something about her, of course—it was all about her beautiful, glorious self.

What a mess. But Jill had three days to get her act

together. And Amelia *had* looked good. Jill couldn't have stopped herself going over even if she had tried her hardest. There was this pull about her. Looking at her from a distance wasn't enough. Jill had to hear the sound of her magical voice. How low it dipped when she said hello.

The intercom buzzed. Her next client had arrived. If anything, Jill owed it to her other clients to let Amelia go. She owed them her full attention, not whatever brainpower she could spare that wasn't occupied with all things Amelia Shaw.

Just as Jill opened the door of the Bondi Pink Bean, her phone buzzed in her purse. She checked the message before ordering a drink. It was Hera, sending a million apologies because she was going to be late, but would do her best to be there as soon as she could.

Jill had been stuck in traffic herself, although she didn't know which direction Hera was coming from or if her delay was even traffic-related. Jill didn't mind. This gave her more time to think. She looked around the coffee shop. This Pink Bean looked quite different than the one in Darlinghurst. When she looked behind the counter, into the face of a short but very buff man, she understood where the difference in interior design choices came from. That man could only be Rocco, Hera's nephew, and co-owner of this branch. Jill wondered what the deal was with their connection to the other Pink Bean. She tried to remember if Hera had ever told her about the details. She could check her notes. This reminded her that Hera was, indeed, a very recent client of hers.

Before she had a chance to order, Katherine walked in.

"Ah, Jill. Hera sent me. She's mortified she's running

late." Kat walked up to her and kissed her on the cheek as though they were already old friends. "She's stuck at a job. A discussion with an electrician that got a bit… sparky. She should be here in half an hour. She asked me to apologize profusely and keep you company."

"That's very kind." Although Jill was very good at keeping her own company. "Does Hera think I need babysitting?" she quipped.

"To tell you the truth, I think she's a bit nervous about meeting you like this." Kat ushered them to a couple of very plush, dark green armchairs by a low walnut table. "Please, sit. Make yourself comfortable. What I can get you to drink?"

"Macchiato, please."

Kat sauntered off. Jill couldn't help but follow her with her gaze. Kat was the kind of woman who drew attention to herself. "She'd find a way to swing her behind just going from chair to chair," Hera had once said of her. Funny that Jill remembered that.

She took the opportunity to glance around again. The decor of this Pink Bean was much warmer than the starker whites and beiges in Darlinghurst. Unusual trinkets were dotted around the place—a strangely structured lamp, a row of teeny-tiny coffee cups in all shades of the rainbow. The chairs were all a different color and shape but still, as if by magic, worked together to create a welcoming, cozy vibe.

"There you go." Kat returned with two steaming cups.

"I've been keeping the Darlinghurst Pink Bean in business with my caffeine consumption alone," Jill said. "I'm curious to taste the Bondi coffee."

Kat looked at her as she took a sip. She waited for Jill's verdict.

"It tastes exactly the same."

Kat nodded. "Kristin's a not-so-silent investor." She

painted on a smile. "We use the same beans and machine so the coffee is of the same high standard."

"*Pink* beans?" Jill half-joked, half-inquired.

"Not in color, but…" The skin around Kat's eyes crinkled as she smiled. "I'm so glad you came, Jill. Hera would never say it as such, but she really admires you." The dimples in her cheeks grew deeper. "I know for a fact she kept seeing you way longer than she actually needed to, just because she likes you so much." She interjected with a chuckle. "I said to her: 'My darling, I had no idea you were so keen to pay for female company.'" Kat laughed loudly at her own witty remark.

Jill agreed that, given Katherine's former profession as a lesbian escort, it was hilarious, although she could easily imagine Hera not being amused by her comment. But she guessed that was how Kat and Hera were together. A true case of opposites attract. Only then did the compliment sink in.

Jill was well aware that Hera's need for therapy had been coming to an end. She had even subtly hinted at it a couple of times. But Jill never pushed her clients out the door. She figured as long as they kept coming, they must have a valid reason for doing so. In Hera's case the reason might not have been therapeutic, but that didn't make it any less valid. Hera being a naturally rather closed-off person, Jill could easily see why it would be easier for her to come and talk to Jill once a week instead of confiding in a friend. It also made it easier to see why Hera had asked her if they could be friends. To deformalize their relationship and see where it went.

"Oh, Kat," Jill said. "I can't see that kind of joke going down too well with Hera."

"She can take it now." She fixed her gaze on Jill. "I guess I have you to thank for that. Well, partially. I'm not entirely unaware of my own charms, so…" She chuckled again, but

Jill knew she meant every word. "I'm glad I have you all to myself for a bit, actually. Hera would be mortified if she knew I was going to ask you this…" Kat's eyes sparkled.

In many ways, she was just like Liz. Born to seduce. Or even more so, born to make ill-at-ease women relax. To give them something they might otherwise lack, for various reasons. Jill could feel herself warming to Kat already. She could feel herself getting ready to open up. She also wasn't born yesterday. She knew very well what was coming next, yet she enjoyed playing innocent.

"Liz and I have been speculating about you. I know she told you about it last Saturday. Liz reckons you bat for our team. However, my money is on something not so… strictly defined."

Jill burst out laughing. "Wow. Are you telling me that you've had actual conversations about my sexual preference?"

Kat lifted a shoulder. "You have to understand, Jill. Liz and I used to be in a completely different profession. We still deal with people, but… well, it's not quite the same, is it? Reading people. Trying to figure out what they like… It gives us an enormous thrill."

"I bet it does." Jill was highly amused by Kat. She wasn't offended in the slightest. That must be another one of Kat's talents. "It's no big deal to me at all. I'm bisexual. I've been single for the better part of a year now, after being in a relationship with a lovely man called Rasmus for almost eleven years." Jill had nothing but fond memories of Rasmus, apart from the breakup. There was no such thing as a pain-free breakup.

"Ha. I mean, sorry to hear about you breaking up, of course. But I knew it. I called it. Liz owes me fifty bucks."

"Seriously? You put money on it?"

"What's a bet without stakes?" Kat said matter-of-factly.

"Did it end badly between you and Rasmus?" Kat's facial expression had shifted from triumphant to serene. Maybe, Jill thought, there isn't a world of difference between being a professional escort and being a therapist.

"It could have been much worse. Rasmus is from Sweden and he wanted to move home. His mother fell ill and he thought the time was right to go back. For the longest time, I thought, if the time came, I'd go with him. After all, he stayed in Australia much longer than planned for me. But then, when push came to shove, I found I didn't really want to go."

"Do you regret not following him? In hindsight?"

Jill shook her head. "No. I knew it then and I'm still convinced now, that it was the right decision for me. Not because I didn't love him enough, because I did, and that was the part that hurt the most. But... I would have had to leave my clients. I'm no spring chicken and I would have had to build a practice from scratch in a country that uses another language, despite most Swedes being fluent in English. I simply didn't want to make such a significant move, even if it meant giving up my relationship. And he didn't want to stay, so, there you go..."

"It must have been hard, though."

"It was. For a while."

"And now?" Kat grinned. "Got your eye on someone new or just biding your time?"

Why was Kat asking? Was she just being nosy or did she know something? The latter was impossible. Jill had only told Vic about Amelia. Despite her best intentions, Jill heaved a sigh. She couldn't help it. Amelia wasn't just a constant presence in her mind, it was as though she had taken over.

"Uh-oh. I know that look," Kat said.

"There is someone..." Jill also wanted so badly to tell someone about Amelia—someone who wasn't her therapist.

She would never, in a million years, have told Hera. She wouldn't have told Patrick. Quite possibly not any of her other close friends either. But here was Katherine, Hera's partner, who was so good with people she had Jill ready to blurt it all out within minutes of sitting down. Jill hadn't even finished her coffee yet. "But, it's impossible. Which makes it all the more enticing, of course."

"Why is it impossible?"

"She…" Jill noticed how Kat gave a slight nod of the head. "She's a client."

"Ah." Now Kat nodded as though she understood. "Has Hera ever told you how Liz and Jess met?"

"I know Jessica was a client of Liz's, but, with all due respect, um"—Jill didn't know how to put this delicately—"my profession is bound by a different code of ethics."

"I bet it is." Kat just smiled. "So, tell me about this woman who's got you so tied up in knots."

"I can't tell you about her. Everything I know about her, I know because I'm her therapist, which makes our conversations confidential."

"Then tell me what she looks like."

"Wow, Kat, I have to hand it to you… you're something else. I can definitely see why Hera fell for you the way she did. You're very… persuasive."

"Fell for me? Christ. She made me work for it like I've never worked for anything else in my life. That includes this coffee shop, for your information."

"She needed time. That's all. Look at you now."

"Stop deflecting, Jill. I know all the tricks in the book. I need to hear more about this mystery woman."

"She's… got this very low voice. I've never quite heard a voice like that. It's utterly enchanting. And her lips. They look so pillowy and kissable. They're just the right fullness, you know." Jill sighed again. She sounded like a teenager fawning over a poster of a pop star. "I shouldn't be treating her. I know that much. There are no two ways about it, but..."

"You find it impossible to say goodbye, because then you risk never seeing her again."

"Exactly." Jill downed her coffee.

"Do you need something stronger?"

"I can't. I'm driving." Jill could really do with something stronger. "Please, do keep this between us. I shouldn't even have said anything."

"Of course." Kat said it as though it was implied from the moment Jill had opened her mouth to speak. "What are you going to do?"

"There's only one course of action. I will find her another therapist and then I will refer her." Jill knew who to ask. Amelia would be a good fit for Jennifer. But she hadn't made the call yet. She'd picked up the phone and dialed but she hadn't let the call go through. She hadn't been able to bring herself to do it.

"Will you try and see her again once she's no longer your client?"

"No, I can't do that."

"Maybe not the day after. Or the week after. But surely, if you give it some time... If you still feel the same about her, then you should. Who's going to object to that?" Kat said.

"A lot can happen in a few weeks; it still wouldn't feel right."

"You're meeting with Hera and she's your former client."

"As friends. There's a big difference."

"Is there? Really?" The door opened and Kat looked up. "Speak of the devil." Her face burst into a huge grin at the sight of Hera. "You're right not to tell Hera about this. I think we both know she can be a touch judgmental about things like this." She shot Jill a wink, then got up to greet her partner.

Jill watched them. The ease with which they hugged. The automatic smiles when they clasped eyes on each other. She tried to insert herself and Amelia into a situation like this—greeting each other after work. Tempting though the image was, Jill couldn't see it, because she knew it was doomed from the very start.

Chapter Ten

"You look like you're feeling better," Dawn said.

Amelia was mainly glad that it was just her and Dawn at the pub after practice. Turnout had been scant and even Sophia had somewhere else to be afterward. "Maybe I am. I don't know." The walk she'd gone on the other day had lifted Amelia's spirits. Although, since then, she had been wondering what Jill wanted to talk to her about. Clearly, something had been on her mind. But then she'd just waved it off. Amelia couldn't shake the impression that something was going on but, for the life of her, she couldn't guess what it might be. She'd have to wait until tomorrow to find out.

"Therapy working?" Dawn, on the other hand, sounded as though she could do with some therapy herself.

"Maybe. A bit. It makes you think, you know. Makes your thoughts go into a different direction than they're used to, breaking out of the endless loop of gloom. Which, I guess, is the whole point."

"Any spectacular breakthroughs?" Dawn sipped from her pint.

"It has made me think about forming that 40+ team again."

"Team? Not league?" Dawn sounded as though she might quit soccer altogether instead of enthusiastically joining the team Amelia wanted to put together.

"A whole new league is too ambitious. I thought I'd start with a team." Amelia leaned a little closer toward her friend. "What's going on, Dawnie? Earlier, during practice, you were the life of the party. In fact, there were times I worried for your health, what with the way you tried to tackle Sophia."

Dawn waved her off. "It's nothing."

"Fight with Cindy? Something going on with the kids?"

Dawn huffed some air out of her nostrils. "I'm just being silly. Don't mind me."

"Last year, I would have taken that answer and moved on, but not today. Not after all the hours and hours you've listened to me going on about how I hate work and how I have no energy left to do much outside of it and how much that has made my life suck…" Amelia tried a smile.

Dawn shrugged. "Hardly anyone showed up for practice and now, for what's supposed to be the fun bit, it's just you and me."

Amelia furrowed her brow. She tried to read between the lines. Had Dawn grown completely tired of her? It was possible, of course. Or she could just be having a bad day. "Do you need me to crack a few jokes?"

Dawn shook her head. "You're rubbish at punchlines, Melly. We both know that." A small smile appeared on her face. "I just…" She exhaled dramatically. "I don't know if I can tell you this." She took another sip of her beer.

"What could it possibly be that you can't tell me?"

Dawn scrunched up her face. "Promise not to judge."

"Dawn, come on. It's me. After all the support you've given me, I'm in no position to judge you." This did make

Amelia wonder if her friend believed her to be a judgmental person, but this was not the time to inquire.

"The reason I'm a bit miffed it's just you and me is not a slight on you, okay? It's about who's *not* here."

Amelia's brain had struggled to put two and two together the past few months. This situation required her to push her worn-out brain cells to the limit. But, again, for the life of her, she couldn't figure out what Dawn meant. It was as though the burnout had given her emotional intelligence a huge hit as well. For this reason, Amelia believed that she would know she was on the road to recovery when she was able to read people properly again. Clearly, that time had not yet come.

"The rest of the team? I think some of them are slacking as well, but it's that time of year, you know. It's like this every year when spring turns into summer. You know it will pick back up again."

Dawn chuckled but not heartily. "I know that. I've been a member of the Double D's as long as you have. I know how it goes. What I'm trying to say is that not everyone on the team has the same motivation as me to show up."

"Look, Dawn, I'm very sorry. I'm not back to my old self by a long shot and I'm going to need you to spell this out for me, because I honestly have no clue what you're getting at."

Dawn glanced at her, then looked away. "Sophia's not here."

"And thank goodness for that," Amelia blurted out. Then the penny dropped. "Oh. You'd like for her to be here." She paused. "Oh!"

"I know I'm being an utterly idiotic middle-aged twat," Dawn said. "It doesn't even mean anything. You know I love Cindy and our life with the kids but, you know..."

Amelia didn't know. Amelia's life was the opposite of Dawn's. "You have a crush on Sophia?"

"I guess you could call it that."

"It didn't come about because I asked you to deflect her attention from me, did it?"

"Nah, don't be silly. I liked her as soon as she turned up. I just like how she is. As though she doesn't have a care in the world. And I know you don't see it, Melly, because you're looking at everything through your black goggles of doom, but she's fit. As in H-O-T. Earlier, on the pitch, when she pulled up her jersey to wipe the sweat from her forehead, I thought I might pass out."

"Oh, shit. Dawn." Her friend was right. Amelia didn't see it.

"I'm not going to make a move or anything. I swear to you. It's just a bit of fun for my weary Mommy brain, to get the juices flowing. I'd been looking forward to shooting the breeze with Sophia, but now she's not here. Did she say she was going on a date?"

"I don't know. I don't think so. Does it matter?"

"No, of course not." Dawn took a large gulp of beer. "Not that she'd ever be interested in me, anyway."

"Oh, come on, Dawn. Don't say things like that."

"Why not?" She took a strand of hair between her fingers. "Look at this? Half-gray and limp as a you-know-what." Next, she pointed at her chest. "And these… look about the same as the pancakes I make for the kids on Sundays." She shot Amelia a glance that wasn't instantly decipherable.

Amelia lined up compliments in her head. She didn't need any extra brainpower to say lovely things about her best friend. "Dawn—" she started, but was cut off.

"Look at you, Melly. We've just had practice and you still look as though you could go out into the night and pull any bird you wanted. All you'd have to do is bat those long lashes of yours, paint on one of those half-crooked smiles, and you're settled. No wonder Sophia's going so gaga over you. Honestly, I've seen her look at you and, I swear, she's salivating."

Amelia didn't really know what to say to that, except that was not how she saw herself at all. But that wouldn't help Dawn much right now. "Are you sure you and Cindy are okay?" Amelia had to ask. She had to know. If something was up in her best friend's marriage, she had to help.

"We're fine. We're just… busy and not really each other's main focus at the moment. With a six- and a four-year-old. This time here, tonight, with you and with the team, is all I have to myself. Cindy has her choir. Between that and the kids, there isn't a lot of time left for the two of us."

"Anytime you need me to babysit, I'm there." Amelia offered.

"Really?"

"I know I haven't really been there of late, but—"

"It's okay. I don't want you to apologize for that. You're not our free babysitting service. I know what you've been going through is no joke."

"Next week. I'll take the kids for an evening. Or a day at the weekend, if you want. So you and Cindy can go on a proper date, sleep in, the works."

"Are you sure you're ready for that? For the record, that is not why I was telling you this."

Amelia was far from certain—minding two children for a day would wipe her out for the next few days. But she didn't have anything else to do. She just wanted to help Dawn and Cindy.

"I'm sure," she said, sounding much more confident than she felt. "Julian's easy. I'll just kick around a ball with him."

"Milly's a right nightmare. It's like the terrible twos have become the fearsome fours." At least Dawn followed up with a chuckle.

"It's about time I put in some decent godmother time." Amelia was already racking her brain for what to do with the kids. But she'd think of something. This wasn't the first time she'd be minding small children, although it would be the first time since her panic attacks.

"You would tell me if you weren't up for it?" Dawn put a hand on Amelia's upper arm. "I'd need to know."

"It's going to be fine. I promise."

"Thanks." Dawn gave her arm a quick squeeze, then went back to work on her pint.

"Does this mean I no longer get to moan about Sophia?" Amelia asked.

"Moan all you want, but don't expect me to feel sorry for you," Dawn said.

"I should say something to her, though. Flattery can only go so far until it becomes massively annoying. I also don't want to get her hopes up in any way, shape, or form."

"Are you sure?" Dawn chuckled. "You don't want to take one for the team?"

"What? Sleep with her so I can tell you what it's like?" Under the table, Amelia hit Dawn's knee with her own. "Wow."

"Just kidding, Melly." Dawn grinned again. "And don't worry. I'll be there for her after you've let her down gently." She fixed her gaze on Amelia. "When are you getting back in the saddle? Now that you're feeling better, maybe you should think about that."

Amelia shook her head. "It's too soon. I'm not ready for any of that."

Chapter Eleven

"What did you want to talk about the other day? When we ran into each other at the Pink Bean?" Amelia asked as soon as they had finished exchanging pleasantries. She looked different—better. Her cheeks were a touch rosier and her eyes had more light than shadow to them.

Jill swallowed hard. She had made the call to Dr. Jennifer Scarpa and wrangled a favor she'd have to repay in the future. However, Jennifer would only be able to take on Amelia as a new client as of next month. Because Jill didn't want to interrupt Amelia's therapy for too long, especially now she seemed to be benefitting from it, she had decided to wait to tell her.

"I'm sorry about that. It was nothing important," Jill said.

"That's not how it came across. It was a bit weird, actually."

"I understand that. It was entirely my fault. Do you think we can sweep it under the rug and forget it ever happened?"

Amelia frowned. "Isn't that exactly what you're not supposed to do in therapy?"

Jill half-chuckled. "Touché" Could this woman get any more delightful? Jill was just getting herself into more and more trouble as the minutes ticked by. "And, yes, of course, you're right." She smiled apologetically. "But it was really nothing. I promise you." She dipped her chin slightly, as though that would make what she was saying somehow truer. "Would you like to tell me about your week?"

While Amelia didn't look totally convinced, she went on to tell Jill about how nice her walk had been the day they'd run into each other.

"I also somehow seem to have gotten myself back into babysitting duty for my godson and his little sister."

"Does it feel like a duty? Like something you need to do?"

"Yes and no." Amelia looked behind Jill, studying the painting on the wall. "I always used to babysit for them, and I've never minded doing it. It's not like I did it every week. Maybe twice a month. I always figured it was a win-win situation because I got to spend time with the kids and it gave my friends Dawn and Cindy a much-needed break. But after I had my, well, I guess we can call it a breakdown, I took time-out from my godmother duties. Whereas Dawn and Cindy, they never get to take a time-out. It just made me feel over-privileged again, which, in turn, made me feel guilty."

Amelia stifled a sigh, then continued.

"When I offered to babysit, I hadn't thought it through at all. I offered because I could sense that Dawn really needed it and because I want to do something nice for her. She's really been there for me. I cried on her shoulder so many times, while Cindy was home alone with the kids. So, the way I see it, it's the least I can do, but it also makes me nervous, while it never used to faze me before."

"Why do you think you're so nervous about it?" Jill took a page from Amelia's book and stared at the bronze sculpture to Amelia's left. It was either avert her gaze or get totally lost in her broody eyes again.

"Because it makes me wonder if I'm ready. If I'm not pushing myself for the sake of pushing myself. You said this was going to take time and now I'm wondering if a subconscious part of me is rebelling against that by doing something I might not have enough stamina for. These are not kids you can ask to occupy themselves, if you know what I mean."

Jill couldn't help but look now. Amelia's lips were drawn into that half-smile again. She nodded and hoped that would be enough for Amelia to continue. She was also completely and utterly aware that she was being the most inadequate therapist ever. Amelia didn't say anything else. She required a prompt from Jill.

"Have you thought about what you want to do with them?" Jill asked.

"I might take them to the zoo."

Did Amelia just roll her eyes. Jill was jolted right back into good-therapist mode. Was it because of her?

"I have grown opposed to keeping animals in captivity. Just as I seem to have grown opposed to a great many other things that I never used to consider. But kids love going to the zoo. In my current state of mind, it's easier to take the kids to the zoo rather than to the playground or entertaining them at home and inventing games for them to play all afternoon. But yeah, I find myself checking my privilege all the time and at the same time I get so exhausted with myself for doing so."

Phew. Amelia was exasperated with herself. Not that this was a good thing, but at least it wasn't Jill's fault.

"Maybe Dawn was right," Amelia said on a sigh. "Maybe I do need to start dating again. Maybe it's the same as with babysitting. Maybe I just need to give myself a push, but…" She grew silent.

Jill still had enough sense to recognize this as a fruitful lull in conversation. Amelia was building toward something. Her brain was making the necessary connections. "You know how I talked about dating myself and self-love and all of that…"

Jill nodded, her gaze firmly fixed on Amelia now.

"For months now, I haven't been able to, um, perform the ultimate act of self-love." She raised her eyebrows. "*You know.*"

Oh, fucking fuck. This was very quickly becoming too much for Jill. The image Amelia's words suddenly evoked was simply too much to handle. "You mean, um, masturbation." She could barely get the word past her lips. Her voice had even croaked a little. This was absolutely no way for a doctor to behave.

"It is okay to talk about that?" Amelia brushed her hair away from her shoulders, baring the pale, elegant length of her neck.

"Um, yes… of course." Jill needed to regroup, but she didn't know how. Her clients often talked about masturbation, of course, and she had no problem remaining cool and professional. But listening to Amelia talk about touching herself had her rattled. She could only hope her cheeks wouldn't flush bright pink. "This is a safe space. You can talk to me about anything." At least the last part had come out believable.

"I can't bring myself to climax. Not that that should stop me from going on a date." Amelia giggled almost shyly. "But my thinking is if I can't even do that, if I can't give myself that kind of joy, what chance do I have of enjoying a date with another person? In the scheme of things? Isn't it a massive hint that I'm not ready?"

Jill shuffled around in her chair. She glanced at the clock. They still had more than twenty minutes together. Should she excuse herself? But how would that look if she did so now, after what Amelia had just told her? "Not, um, necessarily. Maybe, um, a… date is what you need," Jill stammered. She couldn't think straight, let alone ask a poignant question to steer further conversation.

"Jill?" Amelia leaned forward. "Are you okay?" She pushed herself out of her chair and started toward Jill. "You don't look okay." She stopped halfway between their chairs. "Is this a medical emergency?"

"No, no," Jill managed to say. "I might have had something dodgy for lunch, but it's definitely not an emergency."

Amelia took a step back.

Thank goodness. "I'm so very sorry. Could you excuse me for just a few minutes?" Without casting another glance at Amelia, mainly for fear of what it might do to her, Jill hurried out of her office and hid inside the bathroom.

Before she was able to face her reflection in the mirror, she took a deep breath. A deep pink blush ran all the way from her neck to her hairline. How utterly mortifying. But that wasn't the worst of it. Jill was being unprofessional in the most inexcusable way.

She splashed some cold water on her face, hoping it would cool down her skin, which looked like she'd been out in the afternoon sunshine without sunscreen for hours. What was next? Breaking out in hives? Maybe this was a medical emergency, after all. Maybe Jill's purely physical reaction to Amelia was so fierce that—

"Stop it," she told her reflection. She ran a hand through her hair, tucked a few strands behind her ears. "Get a grip." It was easy enough to say. And Jill really needed to hear it. But she still had to go back in there. She still had to face Amelia.

Why had she ignored her own and Vic's advice? But this wasn't a matter of simply following advice. There was something special in the air whenever she was with Amelia. She felt it shimmer between them. Yes, it made her act foolishly and impulsively, but it also made her feel alive. It might be unethical, but, so far, it had proven impossible for Jill to give up her sessions with Amelia.

She could disturb Patrick's session and ask him to apologize profusely to Amelia and send her home, but that would just delay the problem. And she'd have to answer to Patrick. Interrupting a session was only permissible in an actual emergency situation. The only thing in acute distress was Jill's heart—and, perhaps, her ego. And maybe some other body parts as well.

She stared into her own blue eyes. "This. Is. Ridiculous," she told herself. Wasn't that part of the very definition of a crush on another person, though? She took another deep breath and went back to her office.

Chapter Twelve

AMELIA'S BRAIN might not be in optimal shape, but she knew something was going on. First, there was Jill's refusal to address her bizarre behavior of a few days earlier. And now this? Just as Amelia was talking about something so delicate —something not very easy to discuss.

She couldn't help but question her psychiatrist's sanity, which wasn't really something she was prepared to worry about. Perhaps it sounded cold, but whatever was going on with Jill, wasn't Amelia's problem. She came here to get better, not to get sucked into another person's issues.

But still, when Jill walked back in, Amelia couldn't help but feel concern. A few drops of water lingered on Jill's upper lip, but she looked more composed than before.

"Obviously, I won't charge you for this session," Jill said, her voice a little unsteady.

"Do you want to continue or should I leave?" Amelia asked.

Jill heaved a sigh. "Stay, please. We should talk."

"That's what I'm here for." For the first time, Amelia

wondered if her trust in Jill was misplaced. Jill's erratic behavior was a bit unnerving.

"I don't really know how to say this." Jill fidgeted with the sleeve of her blouse.

Amelia took another good look at Jill. She might look more composed than before, but she still seemed out of sorts. She let the researcher in her take over and regarded the situation from a scientific point of view. Jill had behaved weirdly when she'd run into her. Jill had acted all coy and evasive when Amelia asked her about it. Jill, then, got completely flustered when Amelia admitted to failing to get herself off. Whatever Jill was about to say next, if she could ever get the words past her throat, should be very interesting indeed. At the very least, Amelia's powers of deduction were coming back to life. Her brain was waking up. Although, surprisingly, that wasn't the most exhilarating sensation coursing through her.

"I owe you a massive apology, Amelia. I've been profoundly unprofessional."

Amelia waited.

Jill only managed to look her in the eye for a brief moment.

"This is extremely embarrassing to admit, but, um…" She rubbed a finger over her chin. "I have inappropriate feelings for you. For that reason, I should no longer be your therapist."

Fucking hell. Suspecting it was one thing, hearing Jill say it out loud was something else entirely. "Inappropriate?" was all Amelia could mutter.

"I shouldn't have feelings for you at all, except for wanting the best for you. I've spoken to a colleague, an excellent psychiatrist. She has agreed to take you on as a client, although she only has an opening for you next month."

"Wait. You're saying that I need to get a new therapist?"

Jill nodded.

Amelia guessed that asking if Jill couldn't just get over it was not the best thing to say next. She huffed out some air.

"I'm sorry," Jill said. "You didn't ask for this and I know it's a nuisance." Jill rubbed her palms on her jeans. "Oh, fuck, this is so humiliating." She buried her face in her hands. "My professional pride has just plummeted way below zero."

"But Jill, you're such a good therapist. I was feeling better already and I've only been here twice."

"Thank you. That's lovely of you to say, but…"

"I know this is very selfish of me, but is it really necessary for you to stop seeing me? I really don't feel like starting over. What if I don't like this other psychiatrist and I need to find another one and the cycle goes on and on…" Amelia puffed up her cheeks. She knew it was very self-centered, but she had believed that therapy was one of the very few times that she could be exactly that. This was supposed to be all about her. That was the whole point.

Jill half-chuckled. "It wouldn't be in your best interest."

"I disagree." Amelia looked Jill in the eye, hoping to learn the truth. "Or would it be too hard for you?"

"It would be a challenge." Jill held her gaze. "We'd both be constantly second-guessing my motives. And it would just be ethically wrong."

"But aren't you trained for situations like this?" Amelia had a little trouble averting her gaze. Was this amusing her? It *was* a boost to Amelia's self-esteem. "Look, I promise you, once you get to know me better, whatever feelings you have for me will quickly evaporate." Amelia was only half-joking.

Jill sunk her teeth into her bottom lip. She didn't say anything.

"Maybe we can try?" Amelia wasn't sure why she was pushing for this. She most definitely didn't feel like seeing another therapist, but she also felt for Jill, who had found the courage to confess her feelings. Amelia was bright enough to know how this complicated the already complex relationship between therapist and client. "Or maybe you just need a bit of time?"

"I would be committing a grave professional error. I would be risking my career and reputation."

"Why? You wouldn't be doing anything differently."

"To put it very simply: it's just not right." Jill swallowed visibly.

"It's not that I don't understand, but, um… yeah."

"I know. I'm sorry. It's hard for you. You didn't ask for this. It's unfair in many ways, but it's how it is. For what it's worth, I think you will like Dr. Scarpa. She's highly capable and has helped many clients who have suffered from burnout. I wouldn't send you to her if I wasn't certain you would get excellent care."

"I guess I have no choice." Amelia narrowed her eyes. Her time with Jill was almost up so this might be her only chance to indulge her curiosity. "Before I leave, may I ask what type of 'inappropriate feelings' you have for me?"

"You may ask…" Jill flicked the tip of her tongue over her lips. "We're officially off the clock. Whatever's said next, is not part of any therapy session. Okay?"

"Sure." Amelia really wanted to hear what Jill was going to say next. "You're no longer my therapist." This was getting very surreal. And what was up with all these women —first Sophia and now her therapist—with their feelings for her? Did the dark cloud she'd been living under make her look extra attractive in some twisted way?

"I know you can't see it now, Amelia, because of how you feel, and that's completely normal." Jill's voice was dead serious. "But that doesn't mean that I don't see the passion you have for so many things trying to find a way out. It might all be a bit hazy right now. You don't really have a clear idea of what to do yet, or how to get yourself going again. But I have full faith that you will. It's as if I can look into that future where you've put yourself together again, and I can see who you will be. If that makes any sense at all."

First, Amelia was stunned by what she'd just heard. Then, she felt moved. Something behind her eyes twitched. If an accomplished, albeit slightly discombobulated woman like Jill believed in her so easily, surely Amelia could find that belief in herself again? "That's so kind of you to say."

"Sometimes, we have to imagine our future self in order to become her."

Something twisted inside Amelia. She would really miss not having Jill in her life. "Did you, um, have any plans for asking me out?" she blurted out.

"I wish I could, but I'm afraid that won't be possible either."

"What if I ask you?"

Jill painted on a grin but didn't immediately reply.

"Would you say no?" Amelia pushed.

"I would, because, again, it simply wouldn't be right. There are very clear guidelines about that. Therapists should never date their clients. The conflict of interest is always too big."

"You only had me as a client for two sessions. We barely scratched the surface."

"That might be so, but… that doesn't magically make it right. You came to me for help. For me to offer anything else, would be highly inappropriate."

"What if I run into you in a coffee shop, like the other day? Would you not sit with me?"

Jill shook her head lightly. "Why are you asking me this?"

"I don't know. I just… I'm genuinely sad about this. I looked forward to coming here. To seeing you. Maybe I'll miss you."

"I understand that completely. The transition might be a little rough, but I can brief Dr. Scarpa, so it doesn't feel like you're starting from scratch."

"I need to meet her first. See how it goes." Amelia allowed herself one last question. "Are you going to miss me?"

"What do you think?" Jill shot her a look so withering, Amelia felt the sheer heat of it course up her spine.

"Maybe we'll meet again someday." Amelia rose. She glanced around Jill's office one last time. "I hope, um…" She didn't really know how to say her final goodbye. She could hardly wish that Jill would forget about her and move on from her crush.

"What you said earlier." Jill stood as well. "About me getting over my feelings for you quickly once I got to know you better…"

"Hm." When they were upright, Amelia had to glance down to meet Jill's gaze.

"I don't believe that for one second," Jill said. "On the contrary."

Amelia couldn't help but wonder what might have happened if she had met Jill under different circumstances. Back in the day—was it years ago?—when Amelia still frequently dated, she might have been attracted to a woman like Jill. Maybe for that reason, out of an instinct that she used to have and enjoy, Amelia reached out her hand.

She glanced at it, hovering in the air between them. Then, Jill, too, extended her hand, and ever so briefly, their fingers met.

Chapter Thirteen

After her last client had left, Jill waited for Patrick. Although no part of her felt like doing so, she had to tell her colleague what had happened with Amelia.

Jill looked at her hand, at the fingers that had touched Amelia's. She could still feel the sizzle the touch had sparked across her skin.

When Patrick entered the small kitchen, Jill made him an inadequate espresso, at least compared to the coffee next door, and humiliated herself further by telling her partner in the practice why she'd had to let go of her newest client.

"I must admit, Jill, I can only admire your professionalism," Patrick said after Jill was done talking. "I can't sit here, look you in the eye, and swear I would have done the same."

"Really?"

"Maybe it's different for me. I don't know. I consider myself a pretty conscientious guy, but if you were to ask me if I've ever had feelings for a client, I could only say yes. It happens. We're only human."

"There's feelings and then there's *feelings*," Jill said. She hadn't confided in Patrick how she'd had a meltdown in her office earlier. She thought it better to keep that tidbit to herself.

"But you only saw her for two sessions," Patrick said.

Jill nodded. "It was more than enough to know."

"What are you going to do now?" Patrick rubbed the stubble on his chin. "Are you going to see her privately?"

"No, of course not." Jill glanced at her colleague. Why would he even ask? He knew it was against every rule in the book.

"Why not? You've already done the right thing." Patrick sounded as though Jill had only referred Amelia on so she could date her. Clearly, he needed further explanations.

"The reason I'm telling you this is because… I don't know her all that well. Yes, I'm utterly smitten with her after two hours in her company, but, she's still fragile. I can't predict whether she might be litigious. Or something might happen to her in the future, in her further therapy, that makes her turn against me. I'm also not asking you for any kind of permission here, Pat."

Patrick shrugged. "You don't need my permission for anything, but… you should hear yourself. You're coming at this from an angle of fear. 'She might be litigious?' Come on now, Jill. As I said, you've already done the right thing."

"I strongly disagree." Was this the difference between a male and a female therapist? Jill inwardly scolded herself for even wondering.

"I know you probably think you need to hold yourself to a higher standard than most. In some cases, you definitely do, because that's what's required of us. In this case, however, there are many arguments for just being a mere mortal." He smoothed a wrinkle on his shirtsleeve. "I'm not your therapist, but I am your friend and co-worker, and I have to call it as I see it. I'm getting a most distinct whiff of fear." He narrowed his gaze. "Maybe that's one of the reasons you've fallen for her so quickly, because she would always be unattainable. Because you've already convinced yourself you could never be with her."

Jill scoffed. "No." Jill knew very well why she had the hots for Amelia. Her own fear was not part of that particularly heady mixture. "No way, Pat. I have to follow my own rules. I would absolutely love to ask her out." The memory of Amelia asking her out, although purely hypothetically, only a few hours prior, sent a fresh jolt of fire through Jill's veins. "But fraternizing with former clients is not something I do." *Oops.* If ever there was a flagrant lie. Jill had spent a lovely time with Hera and Kat only a few days ago. "Actually, scrap that." She shook her head. "Vic agreed with my course of action, though."

"You invoke 'the rules', Jill, but the truth is that there are no clear-cut rules for this. It's always going to be a gray area."

"What are you talking about? Of course there are rules and they couldn't be clearer. There's nothing murky or gray about them."

"How about this." Patrick leaned forward, placing his elbows on his knees. "Let's meet again in a few days. Let's have the same conversation after we've both slept on this for a few nights. We'll take it from there." He rested his kind, brown gaze on Jill. "But promise me you won't beat yourself up over this too much. I appreciate you telling me, even though you didn't have to. I'm talking to you as a friend here and not as your business partner. Be kind to yourself, Jill. I know that breaking up with Rasmus wasn't as painless as you've made it out to be. I know it hurt you that he went back to Sweden."

Why was Patrick talking about Rasmus now? This had nothing to do with Jill's ex. She barely even thought of him these days. Maybe because her mind was so firmly on

Amelia. A sadness pierced through her at the thought of never seeing her again. But just as she had done with Rasmus, Jill would get past it. After all, she'd only spent a few hours in Amelia's company. She'd spent years with Rasmus. It wasn't even comparable. Jill just needed to gain some perspective. What she didn't need was Patrick, in any way, shape, or form, encouraging her to go out with Amelia. What was he thinking? The mere mention of it was utterly reckless.

Jill waved off Patrick's comment about Rasmus. She appreciated his kindness, and she could see where his suggestion to step away from the situation for a few days came from, but she didn't agree with any of the other things he had said. But at least she had told him. That was all that could be expected from her.

"How's Miriam?" she asked. "We should get together soon. It's been too long."

"Have I told you that she wants to go back to school? She wants to get a sociology degree."

"Great idea."

"I told her that getting laid off, painful though it was at the time, might be the best thing that happened to her." Patrick rose. "Speaking of, if it's okay with you, I might call it a day and get home to my wife."

"Give her my best and tell her I'll hopefully see her soon."

Patrick rinsed their cups and put them in the small dishwasher they had agreed on purchasing for the office, after it was evident neither one of them was very good at washing dirty coffee cups.

Jill stayed in the kitchen a while longer, pondering her day. It wasn't just that it wasn't ethical to ask Amelia out. What was even more crucial was that Amelia, by her own admittance, wasn't ready to date. She had told Jill today. It was what had directly led to Jill losing it. Yet another reason why Jill could never face Amelia again. The shame of going to pieces right in front of her, as she talked about something so intimate, was still at the forefront of her mind. Jill had to shake it off now—and she was determined to try—but it would be a while before she was fully back to her former self again.

Chapter Fourteen

AMELIA HAD DRAGGED herself out of the house. She had thought of telling a white lie and using her babysitting duties as an argument to get out of tonight. She'd heard Cindy's choir sing before. It wasn't really something to give up an evening in the couch for. But Cindy was Amelia's friend, too. And Amelia had barely been out at all this week. She no longer had therapy to go to. She'd only been to soccer practice, which had been an even bigger dud than last time, because this week, even the coach, Kate, had been absent. They'd played a lackluster game of three against three, making Amelia wonder about the future of the team. If the Darlings' numbers were already dwindling, how could she ever hope to put together a brand-new team?

Nor had Amelia contacted the new psychiatrist yet, even though she knew that she should. Despite being cut short, she had already benefitted from the small amount of therapy she'd gotten. She knew she needed to continue. But the new doctor could only see her next month, anyway. So what was the rush?

It felt strange to be walking to the Pink Bean, which apparently held all sorts of different open mic nights. Tonight's event was aimed at recruiting new members for The Queer Melodies, the choir Cindy belonged to and was also the leader of. It felt strange because it was also the route to Jill's office.

As if she'd somehow sensed Amelia was about to arrive, Dawn was standing outside, talking to someone who was half-hidden by the coffee shop door. Amelia waved at her, but Dawn didn't even see her—so much for anticipating Amelia's arrival. As she got closer, she understood why. Dawn was in deep conversation with Sophia. Dawn had invited everyone on the team to stop by tonight, undoubtedly to be in Cindy's good books. But Amelia doubted Cindy knew why she was talking outside to Sophia with such enthusiasm.

Amelia thought she could see Sophia's eyes light up when she spotted her. She hoped Dawn hadn't noticed. For crying out loud, she inwardly scolded herself. This was all far too ridiculous. Amelia greeted her teammates.

"However lovely it is to see you," Sophia said, pushing her legs together, "I'm about to burst. I'll be back in a jiffy." She hurried inside, leaving Amelia alone with Dawn.

"Where's your lovely Mrs?" Amelia asked.

"Inside, preparing the troops. You know what she's like at things like this."

Amelia gave Dawn a look but didn't say anything.

"Hey." Dawn leaned closer, in a conspiratorial fashion. She pointed at the silver plaque on the wall next to the Pink Bean. "Isn't your therapist's name Jill Becket? Is this where, you know—"

Amelia nodded, even though she was no longer seeing Jill. She hadn't told Dawn they had parted ways. Something told her it was better to keep Jill's secret safe.

"Do you reckon she'll be here tonight? And if so, whether she would be up to joining the choir?" Dawn asked.

It wasn't entirely implausible for Jill to be at the Pink Bean open mic night. For all Amelia knew, Jill lived above her practice and liked to come down for a cup of tea before bed. The fact of the matter was that Amelia knew next to nothing about Jill—apart from Jill's inappropriate feelings for her. Although Jill didn't seem the type to join a ladies choir, looks could be deceiving and she might love belting out a tune or two.

"No idea." Amelia peered through the window to see if she could spot Jill. What would she even say to her? Still, only this morning, the memory of their fingers touching had sprung up on her when she was washing her hands. Amelia spotted the barista who had served her coffee the other day, but no Jill. "But maybe I can recruit for my new team as well."

"About that," Dawn said. "If you go ahead with that, it would mean leaving the Darlings. We started that team, Melly. You and me. Are you sure you want to quit?"

"It's a tough one. But lately, I've felt out of place more often than I would like." Maybe, it dawned on Amelia, this was down to how she had been feeling more than to the current composition and average age of the team. "Do you sometimes feel like that?"

With the corners of her mouth firmly pointed down, Dawn shook her head. "Can't say that I do. Sure, twenty-somethings like Sophia can run a hell of a lot faster than I do, but they don't have my experience on the pitch. This isn't a pro league where you're forced out after turning thirty-five." She scrunched her lips together. "Maybe we just need to persuade a few more women of our age to join the Darlings, in order not to feel so old, in comparison." She followed up with a chuckle. "Although, I'm not claiming we're old at all."

Amelia nodded. "Maybe."

"Think about it, Melly." Dawn glanced inside. "Sophia never came back."

"How's that going?"

"She was quizzing me about you, actually. So, yes, she still has the hots for you." Dawn sighed. "That's my only currency with her: information about you."

"What did you tell her about me?" Amelia arched up her eyebrows.

"Nothing intimate." Dawn smirked. "I promise."

Someone from the choir, recognizable by the white blouse she wore, ushered the people from the sidewalk into the coffee shop. Sophia had saved seats for Amelia and Dawn.

"Can we talk later?" Sophia whispered in her ear.

"Sure." It was time to spell it out in terms that could no longer be misunderstood. Although, perhaps, Amelia had been enjoying Sophia's attention. Maybe it had contributed to her feeling better—until her shrink had dropped her.

Cindy introduced The Queer Melodies and told the audience that they were always looking for new members. She touted the advantages of singing in a group, a few points of which Amelia had researched for her. She couldn't have her friend give out information that wasn't scientifically verified.

As the choir sang, Amelia scanned the Pink Bean. Behind the counter, a mature Asian woman was pouring wine. What a fun coffee shop, Amelia thought, to serve coffee by day and wine by night.

When she glanced outside, she spotted a woman with shoulder-length gray hair and a vest. Amelia's gaydar pinged. Just as the song was reaching its big climax, Amelia saw how the woman outside waved someone over. From the looks of it, many people had some recruiting to do this evening. Another woman stepped into view. A woman that looked very familiar to Amelia. She wasn't sure, however, if she wanted the woman in the vest to succeed in her particular audience recruitment. It could make for a rather uncomfortable rest of the night.

Chapter Fifteen

JILL GREETED SHERYL. It wasn't the first time she'd run into her on the street outside her office. Tonight, Sheryl was trying to entice her to join one of the Pink Bean open mic nights.

"It's a choir," Sheryl said. "They've only just started. I'm here to quietly usher in any stragglers."

While Jill considered the offer, Sheryl added, "There's wine and, apparently, we also have a bunch of female soccer players in. The choir leader's wife is on the team." Sheryl waggled her eyebrows as though that was the kind of information that would tip Jill over the edge. Little did Sheryl know that the mention of female footballers made Jill's ears perk all the way up. Might Amelia be here tonight? And if so, was it a good idea for her to go inside?

"I have work to finish at home," Jill said. Her head knew she really shouldn't set foot inside the Pink Bean tonight—the rest of her could hardly be stopped.

"Oh, come on, Jill. Live a little. Kristin will be chuffed to see you. Not to be blunt, but apart from work, what or who is waiting for you at home that's so terribly exciting you'd miss a beautiful choir singing angelic songs?"

Jill didn't know Sheryl all that well, but she did know she could be very persuasive. However, from what Jill could hear from inside, the choir members' voices weren't all that angelic.

"Okay. Wrong argument." Sheryl took a step back, as though wanting to let Jill pass.

With the possible prospect of Amelia being inside, Jill didn't need a lot of persuading. Even if the chances of Amelia being there were only 50/50, Jill wanted to go in. It wasn't a rational decision by any means. It certainly wasn't ethical. But that didn't mean Jill didn't want it as badly as anything she'd ever wanted.

"You had me at hello." Jill let Sheryl guide her in.

They sneaked behind the gathered crowd and made their way to the counter. From her new vantage point, Jill scanned the audience. Almost all of the tables were filled. She recognized a few faces she sometimes encountered at the Pink Bean, but no one she had any sort of relationship with.

Sheryl offered her a glass of wine. She held up the glass of sparkling water with lime she had in her own hand. "Apologies to your ears. I don't know why Kristin didn't make them audition before letting them sing here." She sent her a crooked smile.

After having taken a sip, Jill resumed her scanning of the audience. Almost instantly, her breath stalled.

Amelia was looking straight at her. Jill's heart thud-thudded in her throat. Her chest felt like it might explode. The iffy choir soundtrack faded into the background. Jill took another sip. Amelia must have seen her and Sheryl sneak in. Had she followed her with her gaze? What was she thinking? Jill hoped Amelia didn't conclude that Jill was stalking her or something outrageous like that. It was perfectly plausible that she would be here tonight, what with her office being next door.

Jill tried a smile accompanied by a small nod of recognition. Amelia smiled back, although Jill wasn't sure she could classify it as a smile. It came across as a touch forced. Oh, Christ. Jill was making a right tit of herself once again. What was it with this woman? Jill couldn't remember ever feeling this silly, so out of control of her emotions before. It was as though Amelia had this hold over her, made her go a little unhinged when she was near. At least she knew she had made the right decision by ending their therapist-client relationship. That was a definite no-go. Jill stood there, her gaze glued to Amelia's half-smiling, pillowy lips, her ears wanting nothing more than to hear her improbably sultry voice again. It was obvious she could never offer Amelia anything in the way of counseling again. If anything, Jill could very much do with a bit of counseling herself.

When the song stopped, Sheryl asked, "Are you okay, Jill? You look like you've seen a ghost."

Jill looked away from Amelia. "I'm fine." She took another sip of wine.

"If you're sure." Sheryl pointed at a free table toward the back. "Do you want to grab a table?"

If she did, Jill wouldn't be able to spy on Amelia anymore, which, surely, made it the right thing to do. "Sure." Again, she followed Sheryl.

The choir started up again. Jill was glad that silence was required from the audience. Her voice would betray her, just like her face had done so earlier. Being near Amelia was such an excruciating but exciting challenge.

Jill took the time the song lasted to figure out, if she had the opportunity, what she would say to Amelia and, more importantly, how she would keep her cool. She had low aspirations for the latter.

The song ended and the woman at the front said that they would take a break, during which they would be available to speak to anyone interested in joining the choir.

"They're recruiting," Sheryl said. "Interested?" She had one eye on the counter. "I predict a run on booze more than people signing up to join. Are you okay here on your own? I'm going to lend a hand behind the counter."

"Of course," Jill lied. "No problem." Then she found herself alone, unprotected by another person's company. She could only see the back of Amelia's head. She was talking to a younger woman. From the younger woman's body language—her chest fully turned toward Amelia, her chin dipped low—Jill could pretty easily deduct that she was interested in more than Amelia's friendship. Jill's first thought was that the other woman must be Sophia. Her second thought was that she shouldn't know this. She looked a little closer. She couldn't help herself. Were Amelia and Sophia here together because they were on a date or because they were on the same soccer team? The prospect of the former made something in Jill's stomach contract. For crying out loud. Was she jealous now? She rolled her eyes at herself—at her own utter foolishness.

She took a deep breath and let the air escape from her lungs slowly in a bid to get a grip. If she wanted to, she could leave. All she had to do was get up and walk out. She would pop in tomorrow and let Sheryl know that she'd had to leave. It was as easy as that. But as long as Amelia was sitting a few tables away from her, Jill was staying put.

The woman who Jill thought was Sophia stood and made her way to the counter. Not long after, Amelia turned around, and looked straight at Jill again. What should she do? Jill gave a limp wave, which didn't make her feel any less ridiculous. Should she go to her? Have a quick, polite chat? Was that even an option?

The decision was made for her. Amelia walked toward her. Jill didn't even have time for another relaxing deep breath.

"Hey," Amelia said, her voice low and easy. "Is this okay? For me to come talk to you?"

"Of course. We can hardly pretend to be strangers." Jill's palms were going clammy. "Would you like to join me?" The chairs around the small table were much closer to each other than the chairs in Jill's office.

Amelia sat and glanced at Jill from under her lashes. "I, uh, wanted to thank you for what you said the other day, about you being able to see what I'll be like again once I'm over this burnout. I've been mulling it over. Even though I'm not there yet by a long shot, it was a lovely thing to hear."

It was also incredibly out of order, Jill thought, but she couldn't help but smile widely. The corners of her mouth just pulled themselves up as if Jill had no command over them. "I meant it," she said. There were so many other things she'd like to say to Amelia, but, apart from a Pink Bean open mic night not being the time or place, Jill knew she shouldn't. "The woman you're sitting with," she said instead. "Is that your teammate Sophia?"

Amelia nodded and cast a quick glance at the counter. Sophia was still queueing.

"How did the babysitting go?" Jill asked, just to say something—to keep Amelia in that chair and close to her as long as possible.

"Absolutely fine." A smile bloomed on Amelia's face. "I've missed those kids so much."

Did you ever want any of your own, Jill wanted to ask, but swallowed the question down. "That's great." Amelia might not know it yet, but Jill sensed that it wouldn't be too long before she was back on her feet. All the signs were there.

"Unlike tonight's entertainment." Amelia curtly shook her head. "I love Cindy dearly, but that choir is a mess."

"They're charming in their own unique way, I guess."

"They most certainly need some fresh blood."

"Have you ever thought of joining?" Jill asked.

"Cindy begs me every time I see her, but… I never used to have the time when I was still working. And after work, I was busy with soccer. And I haven't really been up to new things lately, so."

"Maybe they'll succeed in recruiting you tonight." Jill offered a smile. Behind her calm mask, every atom in her body was spinning out of control. This sort of small talk was all well and good, but it was driving Jill more and more crazy as it continued. If she was really, truly honest with herself, what she really wanted to do, was cup Amelia's jaw in her hands, pull her near, and kiss her on those dreamy lips. Jill really had to get a grip.

"I doubt it." Amelia glanced at the counter again. Jill followed her gaze. Sophia was heading back to their table with fresh drinks. "I'd better get back."

"Sure." Already, the euphoric sensation inside Jill was turning to utter deflation.

"Bye, Jill." Amelia rose, took a step away from her, then turned around again. "Are you staying until the end? Maybe we can talk some more after?"

"Yes," Jill said quickly. She had forgotten how utterly exhausting it felt to be this smitten. "I'll be here." And how damaging it was to her self-esteem.

"Good." Was that a flirty smile that Amelia had just drawn her delicious lips into? It was too late to figure out because Amelia had turned away to join Sophia.

Despite desperately looking forward to it, Jill wasn't so sure whether it was a good thing that they would be talking later. She would be turning fifty in a few weeks' time and this was no way for a woman of that age to behave. Nor should she entertain thoughts of kissing other women like that. Amelia had never given her any hints that she might even be interested in Jill. If anything, she'd been flummoxed when Jill had told her about her feelings.

Until, perhaps, tonight.

Chapter Sixteen

The occasion was not the right time to let Sophia down gently. Amelia had tried to steer the conversation in that direction, but during the break, they'd been interrupted by teammates and then there was the small matter of Jill's gaze burning a hole in the back of Amelia's head.

By the time the choir's performance had ended and people at the various tables dispersed, Amelia found her priority was no longer convincing Sophia that they shouldn't go on a date. After their short chat earlier, Amelia found herself wanting to talk to Jill again. It was fairly clear that Jill had not gotten over her 'inappropriate feelings' for Amelia in the week they hadn't seen each other. Of course, Amelia asked herself whether she merely wanted to bask in Jill's blind adoration—because that was all it could possibly be, in the end. It was clear to her that the answer was yes. For a woman in her condition, worn down by life and society's demands, a bit of blind adoration from someone like Jill went a hell of a long way.

Moreover, Jill was an attractive, intelligent woman, who'd had the courage and the wherewithal to tell Amelia she had feelings for her, which spoke to her character and the rules she lived by. Amelia liked people who lived by an internal code. She admired them, because she knew how tiring it could be to take a stand in this day and age.

So, she made her excuses to Sophia and went to find Jill, who was at the counter, ordering a drink. When their eyes met, Jill pointed at the glass of wine she'd just received, then she gestured at Amelia, who responded with a nod. She might as well. It wasn't as if she had to go to work in the morning. By the time she made it past a throng of white-bloused choir members, Jill was waiting for her with a drink in either hand. Amelia eagerly accepted one.

"Shall we talk over there?" Jill nodded at a table in the corner, away from the crowd. "The second act was perhaps a touch better than the first," Jill said, once they'd sat.

Amelia smiled at her and took the opportunity to let her gaze linger on Jill's face. In this light, her eyes were a blueish gray. "Thanks for staying."

Jill chuckled. "I was hardly going to say no."

"Does it, um, feel like you're skirting a very thin line?" Maybe Amelia felt emboldened by having just looked deep into Jill's eyes. "To sit here with me, I mean?"

"I enjoy your company. I think you know that."

"I'm very flattered by that, because I really haven't been the best company lately. Ask any of the women of that rather rowdy soccer team over there." She nodded at a group of her teammates.

"That's surely just the impression you have of yourself. Your new teammate wouldn't be all over you if it were actually true," Jill said. "I could so easily see it when I watched her interact with you. She *really* likes you."

"True." Amelia wished she could go back to the time when another woman's interest in her didn't surprise her so much—a time when the discrepancy between what she felt and reality didn't seem so vast.

"At the risk of making even more of a fool of myself than I already have," Jill said, "I totally understand where Sophia is coming from." She sunk her teeth into her bottom lip—maybe to keep herself from bursting into a nervous grin?

"What are you trying to say?" At least, Amelia was amused by all of this. She was *feeling* something. She was glad she'd dragged herself out. Or was she so happy because she'd bumped into Jill? Why had she asked her to stay after the choir had finished, anyway? And was that even fair on Jill? Nothing was clear-cut here, while this was a time when Amelia needed things to be very defined—just so she could feel as though she wasn't losing control again. But, whereas Sophia hitting on her grated on her nerves, when Jill did, in her own, hesitant-but-here-I-am way, it made Amelia feel like she yearned to lose a bit of control. Probably because Jill had been her therapist, Amelia felt a modicum of safety when she was with her. After all, Jill had let her go as a client, in Amelia's best interest. "That I now have two women interested in me and I should get over myself already?" Amelia's joke muscle hadn't had much of a workout during the past year and her would-be joke landed more as a callous accusation.

Jill shook her head. "Of course not."

Amelia held up her hand in apology. "I'm sorry. That came out all wrong. It's not what I meant to say. It's just that, even though I've been feeling better, especially during these past few weeks, I still say these… harsh things, while it's not my intention. Like my tongue is playing tricks on me and deliberately translates my thoughts and ideas wrongly." That definitely didn't make any sense, but at least Jill was highly trained. Maybe she could decipher it.

"Hey." She offered a soft smile. "You don't have to explain yourself to me. Not anymore." She brought a hand to her chest. "I'm the one who should apologize for saying what I did. I'm also out of practice when it comes to flirting or maybe I'm so bad at it because I know damn well that I shouldn't be flirting with you in the first place." She drummed her fingertips on the table. "I'm sorry."

"I'm the one who asked you to stay, though," Amelia said.

Jill opened her mouth, but then tightened her lips as though she'd changed her mind about saying what she was about to say.

"What were you going to say just now?" Amelia asked. Jill might feel as though she shouldn't be flirting, but Amelia was enjoying it, and she didn't mind flirting back a little. She wouldn't mind leaning into the sensation of simply *feeling* a bit more.

"Something I really, *really* shouldn't."

"For that reason, I think you should, and I'll tell you why, Jill." Amelia took a quick sip of wine and leaned her elbows on the table between them. "I have no information about you, apart from your confession that you have feelings for me. That's all I know about you. Because of how we met, so this is not your fault, but maybe this is an opportunity to give me another glimpse inside that head of yours…"

Jill laughed heartily. "Are you sure that's what you want?" she asked.

"It's impossible for me to know because I have no idea what you're going to say, but you sure did make it sound intriguing." Oh yes, this was all-out flirting. Advanced. Off the scale. A sense of vitality—much more than merely feeling something—brimmed inside Amelia.

"I was going to ask you if you wanted to go next door, where it's quieter."

"To your office?" A spark of something else, something she didn't dare examine further in that moment, lit up inside Amelia.

Jill nodded. Amelia could see her swallow slowly, as though her throat had suddenly gone bone-dry.

Amelia chewed the inside of her cheek for a second, while she contemplated Jill's question. But maybe the time to stop overthinking every last little thing had finally arrived. "Are you still asking? Because if so, my answer is yes."

Chapter Seventeen

So WRONG; *so wrong, so wrong.* The words flashed like bright pink neon in Jill's brain. She was a doctor so she knew it was impossible, yet she was convinced that if she had a brain scan right now, the words might actually light up on the screen. At the same time, this scan would probably show how right Jill thought things to be. How right that in a few minutes, after Amelia had said her goodbyes at the Pink Bean, she would ring the bell she'd rung only three times before. How right that Jill would buzz her in even though it was long after office hours.

It could not possibly be wrong to feel the way Jill felt when she saw Amelia's porcelain skin and her dark, brooding eyes. When she heard Amelia's voice, so low Jill could almost sense its vibrations on her skin.

Jill switched on her desk lamp and the trendy floor lamp she'd bought when she'd moved into her new office six months ago, then turned off the ceiling lights. This off-the-clock occasion didn't require daytime lighting.

She went into the kitchen, hoping Patrick might have left something good in the fridge to drink, but she found only water. She hadn't invited Amelia for a drink and she could always offer her coffee or tea.

And what else? Why had she invited Amelia here? Because it was quieter than the Pink Bean, sure. But also because Jill hadn't been able to stop herself from flirting with Amelia, and Amelia had most definitely flirted back. This was how the cards had been shuffled tonight. Sheryl had ushered Jill into the Pink Bean. Amelia had been there. Amelia had asked her to have another chat after the choir had finished. Jill had asked Amelia to continue their chat in the much more subdued environment of her office. Cause and consequence. This was simply how life went at times.

In some way, it reminded Jill of the events that had preceded Rasmus leaving. The run-up to it had been littered by a score of unexpected occurrences, yet, in hindsight, they seemed nothing but entirely logical.

Jill paced from her office to the kitchen, her ears perked up for the buzzer. It was a discreet sound because, even though Jill left fifteen minutes between appointments, sometimes a client arrived when the previous one was still in session. But no matter how discreet, and even if Jill were to suddenly go deaf, she'd somehow still be able to hear Amelia announce her arrival tonight. She could probably sense the shift in energy just from Amelia standing on the other side of the door. She could—

Buzzzzz.

There she was. Jill pressed the automatic door release to let Amelia in and waited for her, leaning against the frame of her open office door. Even though she'd just spent time with her at the Pink Bean, Jill's body reacted as though she hadn't seen Amelia in weeks. Something started up in her stomach. Her lips puckered as though they were suddenly on cheek-kissing terms. Of course, they weren't. But Jill could hardly blame her lips for that. For wanting more. She already had much more than she could ever have dreamed of—definitely more than the quiet night at home that had been waiting for her before Sheryl accosted her in the street.

"It took a while to get rid of Sophia. She wanted to go to the pub around the corner for a beer. A few of the team went with her." Amelia shook her head. "The look on her face when I said I wasn't going. You'd think I'd just punched her in the gut."

"I take it you haven't talked to her yet?" While Jill felt for Sophia, she didn't want to talk about her.

"I will. Soon. It's not fair. Even—" Amelia stopped talking. "Let's maybe not discuss Sophia." She looked around Jill's office as though it was the first time she'd set foot in it. "It looks different in here," Amelia said.

"Because it's late." Out of habit, Jill walked to her chair. Once there, she wasn't sure whether she should sit. It would make it all feel too much like a therapy session. So she headed for the three-seater against the far wall. "We can sit here, if you like. Or we can go into the kitchen. Can I get you some coffee, tea, or water? I have decaf in case you're sensitive to caffeine at night."

"Do you live in the building?" Amelia asked, ignoring Jill's questions, as she strode to the couch. God, those legs. Jill should check the Darlinghurst Darlings' Facebook page to know when they played next. She wanted to see those gorgeously long legs in a pair of shorts. She dismissed the thought. Amelia had asked her a question.

"No. I live nearby, though. On the next block."

Amelia sat and slung one leg over the other. She was wearing jeans, which was the only kind of pants Jill had seen her in. "Thanks, I'm okay for drinks," she finally said. She nestled herself in the corner of the couch, her body half turned toward Jill. "You know, earlier, as I approached the

Pink Bean *and* your office, I did wonder if you might be there tonight."

"At the risk of sounding like a therapist," Jill reckoned she could get away with a lame joke, "how did that make you feel?"

Amelia chuckled and it truly was a sight for sore eyes. Her face lit up. Her lips, which weren't plump exactly, just sensual to the extreme, curled. Most of all, her body relaxed. It felt as though Jill was offered a tiny glimpse of her true self—of the person she had been before she'd burned out.

"Seriously?" A smile lingering on her lips, Amelia shook her head. "We're not doing that tonight, Jill. That's not why I'm here."

"Why are you here?"

"Most certainly not to reply to any more of your questions. I'm here to ask you some of my own."

"Fair enough." Jill leaned back into the couch a bit more and stretched her legs out in front of her, one ankle over the other. An informal pose for an informal time. It was probably much harder for her to shake the professional vibe that hung in her office than it was for Amelia. Jill spent the better part of her day between these four walls, listening to clients. "Fire away."

"I didn't come prepared." Amelia shifted her body around a bit. "Let me think." She narrowed her eyes. "I assume you're single?" she asked.

Jill couldn't help a silly giggle from escaping her throat. "Very much so. Yes."

"You never know. Dawn has the hots for Sophia and she's married to Cindy, so…."

"Wait, wait, wait. Your best friend Dawn has the hots for Sophia, while Sophia has the hots for you?"

"Oh, yes. Put a bunch of lesbians together and that's how

it will always shake out." The skin around her eyes crinkled as she smiled. "As the cliché goes."

Jill thought of the group of lesbians she'd been sitting amongst at Liz and Jessica's house a few weeks ago. She thought of the women who frequented the Pink Bean. Was it like that for them? "That's a new one for me," Jill admitted.

"Have you been single a long time?" Amelia asked.

"About a year."

Amelia nodded, as though parsing the information she was receiving before fitting it into a larger pattern. She was putting the pieces of Jill's life together. "How long were you and your ex together?"

"Almost eleven years." Had it really been that long?

Amelia whistled through her teeth. "That's a lot of years."

Jill nodded. A silence fell during which she wondered what Rasmus was up to and how his mother was doing. Had he found someone new? A strong, tall Swedish woman with a high, blonde ponytail who looked the opposite of Jill?

"Forgive my curiosity, but... well, my own track record with long-term relationships isn't that stellar. Although I have seen a lot of friends go through breakups." Amelia sounded as though she was musing more than asking. "Why did you split after such a long time?"

"For the longest time, we both believed we wanted the same things. Turns out that wasn't true at all."

Amelia scrunched up her eyebrows. Jill knew her reply was vague and unsatisfactory.

"Are you still in touch? Did you do that other cliché ultra-lesbian thing and remain friends? Although, for the record, I have personally never remained friends with my exes. It's not a thing for me, but I have witnessed it far too often to not believe the stereotype where others are concerned."

"That's interesting, that you never befriended your exes.

If I was still your therapist, I would inquire further about that."

"But you're not." There was that smile again—the one Jill was jonesing for. Jill was also stalling. But she had to set the record straight. Amelia's response to what she was about to say next could make or break the rest of the evening—just as it could decide whether they would ever see each other again.

"My ex is a man—Rasmus." Jill kept her voice level, decades of experience at doing so came in handy. "For that reason, not many lesbian clichés were perpetuated."

A frown appeared on Amelia's forehead. "Oh." She gave a slight shake of the head. "Gosh, I'm sorry, Jill. How utterly ignorant of me. I just… assumed, you know."

"Please, don't apologize. There's really no need." Jill let out a small sigh of relief.

"There is." Amelia lifted her shoulder, then let it drop again. "In my defense, cognitive decline has been scientifically linked to people who have suffered a burnout." She grimaced.

Jill deflated whatever was left of the tension with the widest smile she could muster. "You tell me you're gay. I confess to having feelings for you. You drew the most logical conclusion. It's really fine."

"It's still more than a little ignorant," Amelia said. "But hey, if you haven't gone off me."

Gone off her? What was Amelia even talking about? If anything, Jill had just done the opposite of that, and she was already so smitten. Oh, wait. Was Amelia flirting again? And was Jill off the hook from having to recount her breakup story?

"Not much chance of that," Jill said, just to set the record straight.

"When, um, did you first feel something for me?" Amelia

drew up her knee onto the couch. From the outside, they could probably easily be mistaken for two friends chatting. But whoever looked on from the outside couldn't see inside of Jill. They couldn't see how the fire simmering inside her was slowly fanning more and more out of control.

"Honestly?" It was a silly question, but it was also a way for Jill to make herself look a touch less foolish.

"Of course." Amelia's voice set something else off in her. Like someone had just poured a vat of oil onto the flames licking her insides.

"About two seconds after you sat in that chair for the first time." Jill pointed at said chair.

"Really? Like an at first sight kind of situation?"

Eyes averted, Jill nodded. She couldn't even begin to explain what it had really felt like. The shift of energy in the room, which she had first attributed to receiving a brand-new client. The knowledge had settled inside her, immovably: that the woman sitting in front of her, was so much more than a client, even though Jill had no power to do anything about it.

"I never even knew that really existed. I always believed it was another clever invention by some marketing department of a movie studio or a publishing house." Despite her rather cynical words, Amelia's tone was full of delight. Maybe she'd never been the desired person in a love at first sight kind of situation.

"And I've always believed I'm not that gullible, yet here I am. On the cusp of fifty, with decades of experience in the human psyche under my belt, crazy as fuck about you." Damn, it felt great to say it out loud. At the same time, it was utterly nerve-racking.

"Crazy as fuck?" Amelia huffed out some air.

Was it a chuckle? Jill couldn't be sure. "It's really the only way I can put it into words right now."

"I probably didn't help, what with asking you to stay and coming here with you." Amelia's voice was so low, the cadence of her words so slow, Jill thought the fire raging inside her might melt her before she could say anything back.

"All I can say..." Jill had to clear something out of her throat before she could continue, "is that, sometimes, you meet someone, and something changes inside of you. Something you never want to be unchanged again, despite knowing better."

Amelia leaned forward a bit. "Sometimes you say things that I find very hard to understand. I hear the words, but I don't really know what they mean."

"I'm just babbling..." Jill looked at her hand. Should she extend it? No. It was too soon. Either way, it wasn't because she was confessing to her crush, again, that Amelia had any obligation to respond. But she was here. They had flirted on and off all evening. But still, Jill shouldn't instigate anything. She had to wait, even if that meant that nothing would ever happen.

"I, um, really admire your honesty, Jill," Amelia said. "And your courage. These have always been important values to me, even though I kind of lost sight of them lately."

Jill bit her lip. She shouldn't be hoping for anything with Amelia right now. This was why, earlier, the word 'wrong' had flashed so angrily in her brain. But Jill had failed to listen—again.

"I know. You're going through so much. And I'm just piling on more stuff to deal with."

"This..." Amelia waved her hand toward Jill. "I don't mind dealing with at all." She flashed a quick smile. "I do like you, Jill, but we both know that I'm not ready for anything. I do want to start dating again, but this... If we were to go out, it wouldn't feel like merely dating anymore. It feels like something else because we're not starting from scratch. Which, in a way, might actually be easier, but I just don't know. I'm not there yet. I don't trust myself to not fuck it up the first chance I get. I—"

"Hey." Jill clasped her hands firmly together so they couldn't reach out to Amelia of their own accord—she wouldn't put it past the desire burning inside of her to play a trick on her. "If anyone understands this, it's me. It's okay. I'm glad I had tonight. It was more than I could ever have hoped for."

Amelia let her knee drop off the couch and sat up straight. "On that note, maybe it's time for me to go home."

Chapter Eighteen

AMELIA'S HEART beat in her throat. Could confusion be felt in the blood? No, of course not. Could warring desires provoke a sudden spike in high blood pressure, then? Amelia had read about much more far-out occurrences in the scientific periodicals she subscribed to. As she straightened her posture, her head swam. There could be any number of reasons for it, but Amelia had to logically conclude that the real reason was the conversation she'd just had with Jill.

Either way, she had just announced that she was leaving, so she should at least do that—make a start on heading toward the door. If only her legs would cooperate. Come to think of it, not many of her muscles seemed keen to take her home.

"Are you okay?" Jill asked, keeping a respectful distance. She had done so all night, at least with her body. Maybe not with her words—they had made serious advances toward Amelia.

"Could I have some water, please?" This would give Amelia time to take a few deep breaths and gather her wits.

Jill hurried out of the office.

While she was alone, Amelia tested her legs. She could stand up just fine. With Jill out of the room, the sensation of light-headedness seemed to have left Amelia as well. She inhaled deeply through her nose and exhaled through her mouth a few times. Amelia's body had reacted unexpectedly before during this period of burnout, giving her enough sense to take things easy.

Jill returned with a glass of water. "Do you live far from here?"

"A ten-minute walk tops."

"Do you want me to get you an Uber? Or walk you home if you need the fresh air? Just to be sure." Jill's voice was full of concern.

Amelia wasn't sure being in Jill's company longer was what she needed. An Uber would be the correct choice. But making the correct choice wasn't really at the top of her list, it would appear. She drank from the water Jill had offered her. "Burnout is no joke," she said by way of an explanation. "It's so physical. As I'm sure you know. But before I actually suffered from it, I believed it was purely mental."

"Why don't you sit for a bit." Jill made to put a hand against Amelia's arm, but retracted it before it could touch her. "Come on. You're absolutely right. This is no joke. I'm a doctor. I can't let you leave like this."

Amelia fell back onto the couch.

"Does this happen a lot?" Jill asked.

"It's been a while. I've been feeling a lot better, but…"

"I was probably being a touch too intense with you." Jill smiled, but it was no flirty kind of smile. Although warm, it was laced with worry.

"Maybe I'm not ready for the dating scene just yet." Amelia shrugged. "Doesn't make much difference to me. I haven't been out with a woman in years." She glanced at Jill. She could tell Jill was biting back a question. "It's okay, Jill. You can ask." Maybe sitting here with Jill had been too much for her exhausted brain to process, but it had still amused Amelia. It was the most fun she'd had in months.

"I wasn't going to ask anything." The kindness in Jill's eyes amazed her. "I just want to make sure you're okay. How about I ride in the Uber with you? Deliver you to your doorstep."

Amelia waved off Jill's proposal. "I'm fine."

"With all due respect, I can't accept that. I won't sleep a wink if I don't know you're safe. It's no biggie. I'll take the Uber to my house after. I didn't much feel like walking anyway."

Amelia chuckled. Jill was quite something. Instinctively, she knew not to fight her on this, because she couldn't win this one—she couldn't go against a doctor's advice. "All right. Thank you. I'm impressed with the service of this practice. Given the chance, I will leave you a five-star review." She glanced around the room. "For mood lighting after hours as well. Very cozy."

"Just let me know when you're ready to leave." Jill held out her hand and Amelia gave her back the empty glass. "Do you want some more?" Amelia looked at the glass. Jill's hand was curved around it. So was Amelia's. Why wasn't she letting go?

"No, um, I—" Amelia couldn't tear her gaze away from the glass in their hands. Was this some sort of out-of-body experience? Had she fainted and was she dreaming? Imagining things?

"Amelia." Jill's voice was soft. "Can I have the glass, please?" Jill crouched in front of her. "Are you sure you're okay?"

"I must not be," Amelia mumbled. *Because I'm about to do this.* She leaned forward, slanted her head, and looked into

Jill's blue eyes. Jill didn't move. The glass was still clasped in both their hands.

"Amelia, please," Jill whispered. "Don't make me have to say no to this."

"Then don't." Amelia leaned in a little closer.

Jill didn't pull back, but she didn't move toward Amelia either.

"I want to kiss you," Amelia said.

"You're in no state to make a decision like that right now. I'm sorry. You know how much I want to, but I can't."

As the tension in her muscles deflated, Amelia finally let go of the glass. Jill had obviously released her hold too, because it fell to the floor and shattered into a thousand pieces.

"Ouch." Jill reached for the side of her hand.

Oh shit, she was bleeding. After all this time, when Amelia tried to kiss someone, this happened. Maybe she was still far more broken than she believed herself to be, like the glass on the floor.

"I'm so sorry." Amelia stood, trying to avoid stepping on the broken glass. "Where's your first aid kit?"

"It's just a little cut." Jill examined her hand.

"It looks like a lot more than that."

"Tiny cuts usually look much worse than they are because of all the blood."

"Can I see, please?" Amelia asked.

Jill showed her the side of her palm.

Amelia couldn't get a proper look. "We need more light." She marched to the wall and flipped on what she hoped were the overhead lights. She returned to where Jill was standing and, without asking, took hold of her hand. This was no time for gingerly faffing about. Amelia had to see what kind of damage she had inflicted.

"It looks like there's a tiny piece lodged in the flesh."

Amelia looked a little closer. "I'm really going to need that first aid kit, Jill."

"I'm a doctor. I can deal with this myself."

"But you don't have to." Amelia sent Jill an apologetic smile. If only she hadn't held on to that damned glass in the first place. What had come over her? "I've got this, Jill. I take a refresher first aid course every year. This is nothing. I'll just remove the piece of glass, disinfect the wound, and bandage it. Which would be quite hard to do with one hand, in case you were still thinking of doing it yourself." Amelia made sure her smile was confident now.

At work, she was always the one her co-workers turned to when someone had a little accident. Amelia was also the designated person for emergency evacuations or any other crises. She wasn't cut out to be an idle bystander. In that way, also, this burnout had screwed her well and good, because it had made her feel like a bystander in her own life.

But not tonight. She was going to bandage up Jill whether she liked it or not. Although, if she were to hazard a guess, she suspected that Jill wouldn't mind too much—if the wound wasn't too painful, of course. Years of soccer had increased Amelia's pain tolerance significantly—she wasn't one to double over in pain when a striker hurtled toward her feet-first and collided with her body instead of the ball. She stood and got on with it. Not everyone was like that.

"The first aid kit's in the kitchen. In the cabinet above the sink."

"I'll be right back. Hold up your hand."

"I know what to—" Jill swallowed the rest of her sentence. Amelia hurried to the kitchen. She wasted no time looking around at the decor, but went straight for the cabinet where the first aid kit was kept. She rushed back and assessed the damage. She'd need to get to work with a broom and dustpan after she'd taken care of Jill's hand.

"Do you have a vacuum cleaner here? I want to make sure every last piece of glass is cleaned up. I wouldn't want your cleaning staff to hurt themselves. When do they come in?" Amelia rummaged through the first aid kit. Antiseptic cream. Tweezers. Gauze. This should only take a few minutes.

"Before you get to work on me," Jill said. "Can I ask you to take a breath?"

"Why?" Amelia ripped the tweezers out of their sterile packet and grabbed for Jill's wounded hand.

"You're so… I don't know. Only a few minutes ago you had to sit and have some water. I was going to accompany you home in an Uber. I just want to make sure you're okay before you start removing a shard of glass from my flesh. I'm rather attached to my hands, especially the right one." Jill's eyebrows were arched all the way up.

"It's just adrenaline. Better use it while it's hot." Amelia made a show of breathing in deeply. "Now, can I do this?"

A grimace on her lips, Jill nodded.

Amelia worked quickly and methodically, her hands as unshakeable as she felt in that moment.

"An ER doctor has nothing on you," Jill said, as she studied her bandaged hand. She made to get up.

"Maybe I am in the wrong profession." Amelia shook her head. "Sit for a bit longer while I clean this up."

"Bossy," Jill said. "That's the word I couldn't find earlier. I had no idea you were so bossy."

"It's not because you have a crush on me that you know me," Amelia blurted out. "Sorry. I'm just, uh—"

"It's fine. And you're right. Just another side of you I like then." Jill glanced up at her.

Amelia had almost forgotten that Jill had stopped them from kissing a mere ten minutes ago. Without responding, she made her way back to the kitchen. She left the first aid kit on the table so Jill would remember to restock it the next day. She found the cleaning tools she needed and got to work. While she scouted for glass particles that might have escaped her scouring of the floor, she thought about that almost-kiss again, if you could even call it that.

Jill had been right. Amelia had been in no state to kiss anyone. Fifteen minutes ago, she *would* have kissed Jill for a slew of wrong reasons—not all of them were wrong, though. Amelia liked Jill. But did she like Jill or did she like the fact that Jill was, in her own words, crazy as fuck about her? Most certainly, she didn't like Jill with the same lightning bolt intensity that Jill was experiencing, but that didn't mean Amelia wasn't keen to find out what it would be like to kiss her. By the time she had finished cleaning, she wasn't any the wiser.

After she returned from the kitchen, she plopped down in the couch, and said, "What a night. I could sure use a nightcap right now."

"Do you often use alcohol to unwind before bed?" Jill had a smirk painted all over her face.

"Do you?" Amelia asked.

Jill smiled, paused, then said, "About before... before the glass broke. That was not a rejection, but I think you know that."

Heat rose to Amelia's cheeks. How had she become the bashful one in this equation? "I guess that I... I wasn't thinking. And yes, I do know it wasn't a rejection."

"It wouldn't have felt right for me to kiss you in that moment," Jill clarified.

Oh, the joys of your therapist having a crush on you. "Yeah. I get that."

"That doesn't mean that I'm not immensely flattered by your overture. Flattered doesn't even come close to how I feel. Terribly excited would probably be more accurate."

Amelia felt like she had a decision to make. The glass breaking had been an unfortunate accident, but it had also redressed the balance between them somehow. She weighed her options: either she went home and analyzed this evening to death, or she did something else.

"I think I'm ready for that Uber now," she said. "How about you still come with me and we have that nightcap? Or should I be the one taking you home now that you're wounded?"

Chapter Nineteen

JILL'S HAND THROBBED, but it was easy enough to ignore. She tried to keep her gaze off Amelia's backside as she unlocked the door to her condo. Although it was late, the day was not done yet unfolding its events. She was about to enter Amelia's home—the place that could teach you so much about another person.

Before she held open the door, Amelia said, "It will soon become clear that I haven't really thought this through. I hope you're good at ignoring a right old mess. I wasn't expecting company."

I will only have eyes for you, Jill thought, but even though they'd been flirting, that was way over the corniness limit to actually say. "Don't worry about it."

Amelia led the way inside. She flicked on the lights and dumped her keys in a shell-shaped bowl by the door.

Jill had been expecting near-pandemonium-like levels of disarray, but there were just a few items of clothing draped over the back of a chair and, as far as she could see, some dirty dishes on the kitchen counter.

"What tickles your fancy?" Amelia headed straight for the drinks cabinet next to a giant television.

"What are you having?" Jill asked.

"I think I'll have a brandy."

"I'll have the same then."

"Coming right up. Do sit. Or have a look around, if you feel so inclined. But if you do, be aware that I might quiz you after about what you've learned about me." Amelia's lips lifted into that million-dollar smile again. She brushed a strand of hair from her cheek.

Jill opted to sit instead of snoop. She hoped it would calm the furious beating of her heart. She was still processing that Amelia had tried to kiss her—and that Jill had, for some baffling reason she couldn't even remember, chosen not to kiss her back. Even though she'd been dreaming of nothing else but feeling those lovely lips against hers for the past few weeks. Still, she couldn't complain. She was in Amelia's apartment. There were far worse places to be after dark.

"Here you go." Amelia placed Jill's drink carefully on the table in front of her. "I'll try not to smash this one." She sat rather close to Jill. "Thanks for taking me home."

"My pleasure." Jill reached for the glass with her unbandaged hand. "When I left work, this is the last place I thought I would end up tonight." She took a sip and the liquor slid hotly down her throat.

"And to think that all I wanted was to stay in, for another quiet night." Amelia glanced at her over the rim of her glass.

Something had shifted between them and the shift wasn't subtle. It hung in the air between them, invisible but heavy and glaring, but Jill didn't know if she should say something about it. Maybe tonight was not for that. Maybe it was just for discovering a bit more about each other and seeing where that could take them, if it took them anywhere at all.

"Same here." She held up her hand. "Instead, I end up with this."

"I hope it's not too sore." There wasn't that much concern in Amelia's voice. Jill heard other undertones: flirtatiousness mixed with… something else. Something she either couldn't put her finger on just yet or didn't want to for fear of jinxing it. For fear of finding out that this entire evening had been but a dream and she was about to be rudely awakened.

Jill shook her head. "I know that anything I ask you will sound as though I'm still trying to be your therapist. That's just how it is. But please know that's not my intention." She waited for Amelia to nod. "I am a little worried about that dizzy spell you had earlier."

"I appreciate your concern, but… I play soccer twice a week. I have regular checkups and blood tests. Physically, I know that I'm fine. Mentally, well, I know that I'm not and that I will need more time." She drew up the side of her mouth—even when worried, she looked utterly kissable. "That was the main reason for starting therapy." She interjected with a soft chuckle. "I will continue therapy, by the way. But it's not just talk therapy that's helpful. Being out tonight was actually great. Taking Julian and Milly to the zoo last weekend was exhausting but lovely. Just going for a walk gives me a small thrill again, which wasn't the case a month ago. The rest and the time I've taken away from my job have already had an effect on me. Which gives me hope that there's a definite way out of this."

"Oh, there is," Jill said. "I understand it might not have felt like that for a long time, but I assure you that you will find yourself on the other side of this, stronger and, as you say, much more aware of many things. Of what you want to do with your life and what your priorities are."

Amelia nodded. "I haven't said this to anyone because it's

quite a recent thought and I wanted to mull it over some more before I voiced it, but I have been thinking about resigning. About not returning to Big Pharma. I feel like they took too much from me. They asked too much. Something in me has changed and going back to that industry, for all the good it can do, is not something I want. I think a few months after returning to my old job I'd be right back where I started, because it wasn't just the amount of work and stress and pressure that brought me to my knees. It was everything that's wrapped up in working in the pharmaceutical industry."

Jill was tired, and the liquor was hitting her quite hard—probably because of the decompression after all that had come before—but she tried to listen carefully. "That's a big decision."

"I know." The liquor seemed to have the opposite effect on Amelia. She seemed more mellow but also much more talkative. Maybe because she was in her home, in her safe space. Or maybe because she was talking to her former therapist outside of her practice. "I've no idea of what I would do yet. I've always been paid well, but not enough so that I can retire in my mid-forties. Not that I would want to do that. I need to work. I need to feel useful and like I'm contributing to something."

"You'll find something that you're drawn to." Jill found that most people who wanted to change careers, did when they followed their intuition. Amelia just needed more time to unearth her true desire. To find out where her curiosity, which was still buried underneath the feelings of worthlessness her burnout had heaped on her, would lead her.

"Meanwhile, there's always soccer." Amelia shot her a suggestive look. "But don't worry, I won't try to recruit you for my team again."

"From what you told me earlier, a lot more than soccer goes on amongst the Darlinghurst Darlings."

"Doesn't it always?" Amelia drank again. With her head tilted slightly back and her milky-white throat on display like that, Jill had to shuffle in her seat to remove some tension from her muscles.

"Dawn likes Sophia?" Jill hoped she had remembered correctly.

"Dawn's in dire need of a distraction from her life. Having kids adds so much stress. When Sophia joined the team, Dawn just glommed on to that and she started using that as a way to take her mind off what stresses her, which is her day-to-day life." Amelia paused. "Maybe, for Dawn, her crush on Sophia is her very own mini burnout."

"Maybe you should become a counselor yourself," Jill said. "Help people like Dawn while drawing from your own experience." She wasn't even kidding. Sydney, like any other big city in the world, suffered a shortage of qualified counsellors, what with mental health issues having been on the rise exponentially for decades now.

Amelia burst into laughter. "I've only had two and a half sessions with you." Naughtiness glinted in her eyes, making Jill very curious about what she was going to say next. "Before I got booted out against my will."

"Well-deserved remark." What else could Jill do but laugh at her own expense? Even as a psychiatrist who had trained for years, sometimes, she too could only conclude that laughter was the best medicine. "I happily take it in my stride."

"You are a good sport, Jill. Then again, I did try to kiss your earlier, so... Maybe we're both good sports."

Amelia's glass was empty. Maybe she was one of those people who only spoke their deepest truths when under the influence—or she was someone who talked the biggest trash in that condition.

"Do we… need to process that more?" Jill asked.

Slowly, Amelia shook her head. "Discuss a kiss that didn't even happen? Hell no." She deposited her glass on the coffee table. "Instead, tell me some more about yourself. Why did you and Rasmus split?"

Oh, Christ. Jill was much too tired to tell that story. "It's not that I don't want to tell you about Rasmus, but it's too late. I'm too exhausted to go there right now."

"Fair enough. So…" Amelia stretched her arm over the backrest of the couch and laid her head against it. "Have you had many relationships with women?"

"A few. Before Rasmus, I was in a relationship with a woman called Gillian for a few years, which was not confusing at all."

"Jill and Gillian?" Amelia's body shook as she laughed. "One of the perils of same-sex relationships. What was she like? Gillian?"

"We were together a long time ago," Jill mused. She hadn't thought about Gillian in a good long while.

"You're no longer friends?"

Jill shook her head vehemently. "It didn't end well."

"That's such a funny expression, though, because when a romantic relationship ends, can it actually end *well*?" Amelia let her head roll forward a bit. "I won't quiz you about your former relationships any longer." She pinned her gaze on Jill. "Do you enjoy being single?"

"Enjoy is maybe not the right word. It was good to be on my own for a while after an eleven-year relationship. To truly come back to myself. But, personally, and this is different for everyone, I prefer to be with someone. I prefer the magic of a solid partnership, because I do believe there's magic in that. So if your question is whether I'm looking... Well, it took me a while to reach this point, but yes, I am..."

"That wasn't my question, but good to know." Amelia's hand had been hanging off the backside of the couch, but she put it on top now.

Like her legs, her arms were long, and her fingers rested close to Jill's shoulder. To create some distance between them —Jill was starting to feel hot under the collar again—she put her glass down.

"Or maybe it *was* my question," Amelia said. "And I have another one."

"You're full of them tonight." Jill's gaze was drawn to Amelia's hand.

Amelia sat up straighter and, in the process, her hand dropped onto Jill's forearm. It can't have been by accident, because she kept it there, burning against Jill's skin.

"If I were to try and kiss you again." Amelia's voice now sounded like her hand felt against Jill's skin: smoldering and insistent. "Would you refuse me again?" She slid her fingers underneath Jill's hand and took it in hers.

Jill's brain had stopped working. All she felt was Amelia's skin against hers. The word 'kiss' reverberated around the room, bouncing off the walls, worming its way into Jill's brain. "No," she managed to squeeze past the tightness in her throat. *Not for the life of me.* Maybe Amelia was tipsy—or maybe she wasn't. But she had asked her here. And she had asked the question—in words this time. She knew full well how Jill felt about her. Jill wasn't going to say no twice. Not only because she didn't want to, but also because she didn't have that particular kind of *no* in her anymore. Every cell in her body screamed a big fat *yes*.

"I'm glad." Amelia shuffled closer, until her knee touched Jill's hip, causing another eruption of fire in her flesh. Amelia sunk her teeth into her bottom lip, making her mouth look even more desirable. "Because, as it turns out, I really do want to kiss you, Jill."

Jill pressed her thumb against Amelia's palm. With the back of her other hand, she gently stroked Amelia's cheek. She gazed deep into her eyes before bridging the last distance between them. Before kissing Amelia.

As her lips touched against Amelia's, Jill closed her eyes to eliminate all distractions. So all she could feel were those glorious lips she'd been dreaming of since she'd first laid eyes on them, against her own. Jill hadn't kissed another woman in a very long time and the forgotten softness of it would have brought her to her knees if she hadn't been sitting. These weren't just *any* woman's lips. These were Amelia's lips. And this wasn't a dream. The sensations coursing through her at lightning speed were very real.

Jill cupped Amelia's jaw, her fingertips resting gently against her porcelain skin, as they opened their lips farther for each other. The tip of Amelia's tongue skated against Jill's bottom lip and she eagerly, but still with a modicum of restraint, responded. Jill let her tongue dart into Amelia's mouth, and as she did, she thought she might just melt into the couch.

When Amelia emitted a low groan, Jill pulled her closer. The kiss intensified. Jill gently sucked on Amelia's bottom lip. How had she been able to say no to this earlier? Where had she found the strength? From some secret place she would never in her life access again, that was for sure. Now that she had kissed Amelia, she would never be able to say no again. It was everything she had dreamed of and so much more. That lightning strike would not be undone any time soon. It was wreaking havoc inside her flesh right now. Creating irreversible damage. But Jill couldn't think of any of that. She couldn't let her mind wonder about what this kiss meant. All she could do was lose herself in it more and more as their tongues explored farther and their lips widened more and their hands delved into each other's hair. As this kiss very quickly turned into something else. Something more.

Jill could only hope that Amelia wasn't regretting her decision to do this, because she wouldn't be ready to stop kissing her any time soon.

Chapter Twenty

From the darkest depths of her mind, rising ever so slowly but unmistakably, the flashing red alert appeared. It started with a pulse of light, like the emergency lamp they had in the lab. Soon, the red flashing would be accompanied by a loudly blaring klaxon, the kind that was impossible to ignore.

Yet, Amelia kept touching her lips against Jill's. Maybe, this time, she could outlast the red alert in her head. Maybe even outsmart it. Or, perhaps, even out-kiss it? Because *she* had instigated this kiss. She had asked for it. By god, had she wanted it. So, that annoying, intrusive alarm was to be ignored at all costs. Amelia didn't want this kiss to stop. Jill's lips felt so soft and right against hers. When Jill pulled her closer, Amelia felt it in the pit of her stomach. Although she couldn't be sure if it was a ball of dread dissolving or growing tighter. Amelia had lost the ability to be so in touch with her feelings she could easily name them. This wretched burnout had made her mistake her emotions for other things before. And that was the biggest problem. Amelia couldn't trust her gut any longer. She no longer knew how to tap into her intuition and, on the worst days, she could hardly remember the kind of person she had been before.

One thing Amelia did know for certain was that she shouldn't be in her head the way she was at that very moment. It was a recipe for disaster to think something through while you were actually doing it, especially if the activity you were engaged in was kissing another woman. She could hear Jill's breathing picking up speed. She grabbed for her with more insistence. While Amelia knew very well how it felt to turn on the tap of pent-up lust, right now hers could only let out a tiny trickle. She suspected that for Jill it might be more like a newly breached dam. Oh, for crying out loud. What was she even thinking about? But it was too late. Amelia was lost in her head. Once again, a victim of her incessant thoughts. Even kissing another woman was no match for this worry spiral she was about to plunge into. Of course, she should have known. But the evening with Jill had been so wonderful—apart from Jill's hand falling victim to Amelia's clumsiness—because Jill was such a lovely person. She'd been more relaxed than Amelia had ever seen her. She'd flirted. She batted her lashes at the right time. She'd made something inside Amelia's chest flutter. And then, Amelia had kissed her. Because she had wanted to. The sensation of wanting to kiss Jill along with the very real option of simply doing it had left her a little intoxicated—that and the liquor.

And now what? Jill's hands were in Amelia's hair. Her lips drifted to her cheek, down her neck. All the while, that damned red light pulsed in her head, and Amelia was torn between saying yes and no, although she already knew what the answer would be. If only she could will it into being the opposite. But willing something into existence, into actually happening, that sort of baseless wishful thinking, was not something Amelia believed in—for the simple reason that it wasn't possible.

So Amelia pulled away, preparing herself for whatever look Jill would be responding with: hurt, disappointment, rejection.

"Are you okay?" Jill asked, her voice trembling with worry.

"Um." Amelia didn't know what to say. Her tongue seemed to have lost the flexibility to form the right words. "Sorry."

"I'm the one who's sorry. I'm the one who should know better." Jill took a deep breath. "It's not an excuse, but I'm so attracted to you, Amelia. I might have lost myself in that kiss a bit too much."

Amelia grabbed Jill's good hand. "What are you even talking about? I kissed you, remember? It's me. I thought I was ready, but…"

"What happened? When we kissed?"

"I just… got lost in my head. I was analyzing the kiss while we were kissing. I was in my head instead of in my body and I couldn't stop it."

Jill nodded. "Please don't feel badly about that. It's only—"

"But I do. I'm embarrassed. I'm afraid it will make you conclude that I'm not into you, while I am. Or that I'm not interested in you or that you did something wrong or…" Amelia ran out of steam.

"Don't worry about me." Jill swept her thumb over Amelia's hand. "As far as worrying that you're not interested in me…" She shook her head. "That's really not at the top of my list of concerns." She followed up with a disarming smile. That was often the most discerning quality of Jill's smile. It had the ability to, in a flash, take away some of Amelia's anxiety. "I just want to make sure you're okay."

"I'm fine." Amelia shifted her weight, making sure her hand remained firmly in Jill's grasp.

"I'm not sure you are. Earlier, in my office, you almost fainted—"

"I did not almost faint. I was a little light-headed, that's all."

"Fine. You were light-headed." Jill went silent for a second. Only their breath could be heard. "I'm supposed to know better, but I have to admit that I don't know what to do next."

"You're not supposed to know better, Jill. I asked you here, knowing full well what kind of position that would put you in. You told me in no uncertain terms how you feel about me. I… I guess I used that. I guess I wanted to feel something I haven't felt in so long."

"It's—" Jill started to say, but Amelia stopped her.

"I don't expect you to know anything better than I do. Nor do I expect you to have an answer to what just happened or how to proceed from here. This is why you're no longer my therapist. So we can figure this out together."

"I wish it were that simple." Jill locked eyes with Amelia. "The only reason I know you, the only reason I'm sitting here in your couch, is because you were my client. That will always play a part and I will always feel responsible."

"The reason you're sitting in this couch is because I asked you here and the reason why we're doing all this lesbian processing is because I kissed you."

Jill pulled her lips into a half-smile. "I can see how stubbornness might also be a problem in your life."

Amelia burst out laughing. "Good thing you're no longer my therapist. I'm pretty sure that if you were, you shouldn't say things like that."

Jill scoffed. "You should hear the things *my* therapist says to me."

"You have a therapist?" Amelia sat up a bit straighter.

"I do." Jill glanced down at their hands. "I'm a big believer in therapy; what can I say?"

"Are you in therapy because you believe in it so much or to treat a specific issue?"

"For many reasons." Jill played with Amelia's fingers. "I find it keeps me honest, although that might be an illusion. I find it… unburdening. It also gives me perspective when I need it. As soon as I told Vic about you, she advised me to not keep you on as a client."

"What did you tell her about me?" Amelia couldn't help but ask.

"That's confidential."

"The hell it is." Amelia made sure that the way she looked at Jill conveyed exactly how she felt about that. "You told your therapist about me."

"She's my therapist. Of course I told her about you."

"But I was your client."

"I didn't discuss *your* issues." Jill freed her hand and flapped it around, vaguely pointing at Amelia. "I only discussed my feelings for you."

"And?" This was becoming increasingly fun again. That was also the thing with Jill, there was so much still to discover and doing so was an extremely pleasant way to spend her time—as long as Amelia's head didn't get in the way too much.

"You know how I feel about you," Jill said.

"I'd like to hear it in the words you used for your therapist." And oh my, was Amelia enjoying this.

Jill burst into a chuckle. "I bet you would." Behind them, the old clock Amelia had inherited from her great aunt struck midnight. Jill glanced at her watch as if to confirm the time. "Christ. It's late."

"I can't argue that, but that's a really lame excuse to get

out of answering my question." Amelia didn't want this evening to end. Then again, if she had enjoyed herself more earlier, the night would have effortlessly gone on until tomorrow morning.

"It is. I have clients in the morning." Jill didn't make to get up, however. "But, um, I don't know. Maybe we can see each other again?"

"*Maybe?* You're the one telling your therapist about your feelings for me." Amelia wished Jill could stay. Not so she could kiss her again—she wouldn't be rushing into that again any time soon—but because she enjoyed her company so much.

"Maybe I need you to ask me."

"Okay." Amelia lifted Jill's hand. "Jill Becket, will you go out with me this weekend?"

"Are you asking me on a date?" Jill waggled her eyebrows.

Amelia merely tilted her head.

"I would absolutely love to," Jill said.

Amelia ran a fingertip along the edge of Jill's bandage. "Do you have someone who can change this for you?"

"I think I can take care of that myself."

"If you don't, I'll volunteer my services. I don't have much else on."

"If I need help, I'll call you." Jill gently dropped Amelia's hand, and rose from the couch. "Thank you for a wonderfully interesting evening."

Amelia quickly stood. "Thank goodness for Cindy's choir."

"Oh, yeah. Angel-voiced as they are." Jill shot her a smile, then headed for the front door.

Before Amelia let her leave, she opened her arms wide. "Maybe a hug is the safest option to say goodbye."

"A hug it is." Jill stepped into Amelia's embrace and even though they had kissed earlier, this was the closest they had been so far. Their bodies pressed together. Jill's breath against her neck. Amelia held her as tightly as she could, as though it could make up for having to pull away before.

Chapter Twenty-One

"ANOTHER COFFEE?" Patrick's words were more statement than question.

They made Jill wonder how tired she looked. She hadn't dared examine her reflection too closely in the mirror that morning. Not that she didn't want to look her best for her clients, but decades of experience had taught her that how their therapist looked was often the least of her clients' worries. Jill had noticed it herself when she visited Vic. She didn't go to Vic's to know how Vic was doing. That wasn't the nature of their relationship.

"Yes, please," she said.

"Rough night?" Patrick asked.

"A late one, followed by a lot of tossing and turning." Jill had played that kiss over and over in her head. She couldn't stop thinking about it. She wanted to linger in its memory all day—and for many days to come. What she didn't want to think about was how abruptly the kiss had been cut off. Although the night had ended on a very hopeful note.

"Here you go." Patrick deposited a cup of Nespresso in front of her. "Do you have energy for a chat?"

"Sure. What's up?"

"Not about me." Patrick smiled his therapist smile—inviting but a touch distant. "I wanted to follow up on what we discussed the other day. About your former client."

Heat rose from Jill's chest to her neck. Her blouse, open at the throat, wouldn't be able to cover her body's giveaway reaction.

Patrick, being Patrick, kept the same expression on his face and waited for Jill to speak.

"Circumstances have… changed."

Patrick merely raised an eyebrow.

"Last night, I was with her. I was with Amelia."

Patrick nodded.

"It wasn't planned. She was at the coffee shop next door and we started talking and then, we didn't stop." *And it was just bloody magical.* Until it wasn't. In bed, Jill hadn't been able to shake the prospect of what might have happened if Amelia hadn't abruptly stopped their kiss. "We've arranged a more formal date for this weekend."

"So you've changed your mind since we last spoke?" Patrick asked.

Jill shuffled around a bit. "Maybe… my mind was changed for me." What a cop-out. Of course Jill had changed her mind. She'd only look more of a fool if she failed to admit that to her colleague. "I have to ask myself the question." She paused. "What if I don't pursue this and I let go of what could be one of the great loves of my life?"

"If she is one of the great loves of your life, you won't let her go," Patrick said matter-of-factly. "Sounds to me that's exactly what you're doing. You know my view on this. I won't stand in your way."

Jill waved off his comment regardless of Patrick's admission. "Obviously, I don't know who or what she might become for me. But I feel something when I'm with her.

Something so strong, I can't resist it. She's gorgeous, yes, for sure, but it's more than that. If she hadn't come to therapy... If we'd met in the street or in a bar, I might not have been able to see, and that does bug me, but, in the end, what does it matter how we met?" There was a thought to cling to. Jill was teetering on that knife edge between doubt and acceptance. Maybe all she needed was some time to see the bigger picture—preferably time spent with Amelia.

"Can I ask you something else?" Patrick scratched his stubble.

"Now that you're at it."

"Have you heard from Rasmus at all? Do you have any news from him?"

Jill shook her head. She understood where the question came from. Patrick had been a first-hand witness to the hesitant beginning, the glorious middle, and the painful ending of her relationship with Rasmus. They had become friends and Rasmus leaving, although not a surprise, had hit Patrick hard as well.

"Neither have I." Patrick shook his head. "The first few months, I understood. He had to get his bearings. He probably had a lot to deal with, what with his mother being ill and settling back in. But it's been more than a year since he left and still... nothing."

"Have you tried contacting him?" Jill had stopped trying.

"Numerous times. I've texted. I've emailed. Maybe I should try a handwritten letter next, but I don't even have his address."

"With the benefit of hindsight," Jill said, "I think what happened between him and me might have hurt him much more than he let on and much more than I realized at the time. He didn't get the outcome he expected—he didn't get what he'd been promised. By me. He probably doesn't think too fondly of me, and I can hardly blame him. It could be that he associates you with me and therefore doesn't want to be in touch with you."

"Can I be frank with you?" Patrick asked.

What an odd thing to ask, Jill thought. Patrick was a very gentle man, but that didn't stop him from being outspoken and direct, two qualities she admired in him. She nodded.

"Did you not go to Sweden with him at the last minute because you, um, wanted to be with a woman? With... women in general?"

"No." Jill almost scoffed. "There was no one else."

"I'm sorry, Jill. I couldn't help but wonder because you have feelings for a woman now and..."

Jill cared too much about Patrick to let him talk himself into further trouble. "I'm bisexual, Pat. You know this. I'm attracted to Amelia because of her personality, everything about her, and yes, that includes her physical attributes. Not just because she's a woman." Jill couldn't believe she was having this conversation with her co-worker of fifteen years. She had known Patrick for much longer than that even. They used to work at the same hospital before they set up their private practice together. He'd seen her with women before. He'd met Gillian. "Where is this coming from?"

"I know you're bi. I don't need you to explain that to me. But you're right and I'm sorry. My approach was clumsy. I guess... what I'm really trying to ask is hard to articulate." He snickered. "Not a great feeling to have when you're a counselor."

Jill sympathized, although being a counselor wasn't so much about finding the right words for yourself. It was about helping the client find them as their previous beliefs about themselves got updated and upgraded. But she knew what Patrick meant. In therapy, when you found that one question that broke the conversation wide open, it could really feel like a eureka moment. Patrick had picked the wrong question. It happened. Just because they were both qualified mental health professionals didn't make discussing their private lives —their innermost feelings—easy.

Jill was also curious as to what Patrick was actually getting at. She waited for him to find a better way to ask. While she did, her phone buzzed with an incoming message. Elation soared in her at the prospect that it might be from Amelia, but she had to wait. She was in the middle of a conversation. Looking at her phone now would be rude.

"Okay, let me try again." Patrick shot her a sheepish grin. "Now that Rasmus has been gone for more than a year, do you look back on your breakup differently? Do you think you split for different reasons than the ones you had back then?" He stroked his chin. "Has a new realization about your relationship with Rasmus crystallized over those past thirteen months?"

Patrick sounded as though his anticipated answer to that question was a resounding yes. But the truth was Jill hadn't really been thinking about Rasmus all that much these past few months—and especially not the past few weeks. What she did know for absolute certain was that she'd made the right choice, although it had been excruciating to follow her instinct at the time. The lateness of her final decision hadn't been fair on Rasmus. She'd dilly-dallied for too long. Somehow, she had known that it was over between them. At least, a part of her had known, but it had taken too long for her conscious mind to catch up with that information.

"Goodness, Pat. I might actually be too tired to give you a satisfactory answer to that question today."

"Your answer's not about satisfying me."

"Oh, really? Are you 'shrinking' me?" Jill grinned.

"God no. I wouldn't dare." He pulled his lips into a tight smile. "I'm just genuinely curious. You confessing your feelings for your client made me think about some things."

"Fair enough." Jill smiled back. "I may need to address this with Vic when I see her next."

"You don't owe me an answer." Patrick leaned forward, placing his elbows on his knees. "And apologies if I came across as a bigot earlier. That was not my intention."

You wouldn't be the first nor will you be the last, Jill thought. Being bisexual seemed to throw people off balance. "You're worried about Rasmus," Jill said. "If it's really that important to you, I could try to get in touch with him again."

"Nah. I wouldn't ask you to do that for me. If he wants to get in touch with me, he knows where to find me. Clearly, right now, he doesn't. I have to respect that." He smiled broadly now. "Thanks for offering."

They both looked at the clock at the same time.

"My next client will be here soon." Patrick rose and carried their cups to the sink.

Jill checked her phone. A smile stretched her lips as wide as they would go.

Are you sure you don't need me to change that bandage?

Chapter Twenty-Two

"Wait, wait, wait..." Dawn held up her hand. "Back up, *please.* My middle-aged mom brain cannot compute." She scrunched her eyebrows together to drive home her confusion. "Your therapist dropped you as her client because she has the hots for you. She was at the Pink Bean the other night and you didn't introduce me." An admonishing tilt of the head. "After which, you kissed her! All of this, without me, your best friend, knowing the first thing about it." She whistled through her teeth. "So many lesbian offenses."

"I didn't share this with you for you to have a go at me." Amelia sipped from her glass of wine ostentatiously.

"I will give you all the best friend support you need after I have sufficiently processed what you've just told me." Dawn narrowed her eyes. "I'm trying to remember who I saw you talking to at the Pink Bean that night."

"You were too busy dividing your attention between your wife and Sophia." Maybe it wasn't an entirely fair thing to say, but Dawn could take it. Either way, Amelia wouldn't be a very good friend if she didn't continuously remind Dawn what was at stake in her life.

"Really? Did you notice?" Worry crossed Dawn's face.

"Not really." Amelia had been a bit too preoccupied herself to notice. "I just don't want you to do anything rash. I want you to appreciate what you have with Cindy."

"I do appreciate my marriage. This thing with Sophia… it's nothing. She doesn't even know. I only told you because I needed to blow off some steam."

"As long as you're sure about that."

"How did this conversation wind up being about me? After what you just told me?" Dawn playfully slapped Amelia's knee. "You kissed your therapist. So now what?"

"She's no longer my therapist. She had to refer me to someone else."

"Shit. But I imagine that, now that you're kissing her, you'd rather, you know"—Dawn made an unseemly motion with her pelvis—"than continue therapy with her."

Amelia chuckled despite herself. "It's not as simple as that. When we kissed, at first, it was amazing. Electrifying. But then I got into my head and I ruined it and I put a stop to it before anything more could happen."

"Because of your burnout?" Dawn's facial expression had changed from giddy to sympathetic.

"Going into therapy wasn't some frivolous action on my part. It wasn't a treat to myself now that I'm in my forties to analyze my psyche and learn about my inner workings. It was a step I took after months of hesitating because I had no choice. Because I ran out of other options. Because I needed to change my way of thinking about myself and my life."

Dawn nodded. "Yeah."

"But still, I kissed a woman. That is reason to celebrate." Amelia picked up her glass. "Jill is… I actually don't know all that much about her, but what I do know, I like. A lot. So that's something."

"Hallelujah." Dawn tilted her glass toward Amelia's. "The seal has been broken."

"Well, not quite yet… but something has shifted inside me. It happened so quickly, so suddenly. I can honestly say that I had zero intention of kissing Jill when I followed her to her office, but… when a woman like that confesses to having a crush on you, at a time in your life when you deem yourself most un-crush-worthy, it's flattering. Maybe it's very non-PC of me to admit this, but it raised my self-esteem, and we both know my self-esteem has been in the gutter lately."

Dawn scrunched her face together. "What about when Sophia hit on you? You were totally unreceptive to that."

"True." This made Amelia think. Why had she reacted to Jill by kissing her but been unmoved by Sophia? Perhaps, all along, she had liked Jill a little more than she had realized or cared to admit to herself. "Sophia's too young for me and… I don't know. She's just not someone that…" Amelia didn't know how to continue.

"It's okay, Melly. You don't have to defend your choice to me. It probably wasn't even a choice at all. Maybe, beneath all your feelings of gloom, you already had feelings for Jill."

"Who knows?"

"When are you going to introduce her to your best friend?" Dawn smiled warmly.

"Before I even think about doing that, Jill and I will go on a proper date."

"I'll be expecting all the details."

"I wish I could give them to you already… part of me wishes that first date was over and done with already. I'm ridiculously nervous. I haven't dated in so long and the memories I have of the last dates I went on aren't ones I'm keen to recreate."

"Jill was your therapist," Dawn said drily. "I suspect this

first date will be a bit different than any other date you've been on. Especially since you've already kissed."

"She was, um…" Even though Amelia had ended the kiss before it had come to a natural stop, her recollection of it made her skin sizzle. It made her inadvertently touch her lips, hoping to catch any lingering sensation there. "She came on quite strong. It was a bit much for me."

"Tell her to take it easy." Dawn shot her a quick wink. "What's her romantic history?"

"She's been single for about a year. As far as I know, no serious dating since then. She was in a relationship of more than ten years so I imagine it took her some time to get over that."

"Was she with anyone we might know?" Dawn asked. "You know how these things go in Sydney's lesbian underworld. No such thing as six degrees of separation."

"Oh, um, no. Jill's bi. She was with a man."

"All right." Dawn nodded pensively. "Is she into soccer by any chance?"

Amelia shook her head.

"Singing? Cindy's choir only signed up one new member after their performance at the Pink Bean."

"Not that I know of." As far as Amelia knew, Dawn really liked her wife's choir, no matter their vocal prowess. In the end, it didn't really matter. She and Dawn didn't play soccer with such heart and soul because they were so good at it. They showed up time and time again for the sheer joy of playing, of being out on the pitch with their friends. Scoring a goal was often just the cherry on an already very tasty cake.

"What are her hobbies?" Dawn asked.

"I've no idea, but I'll make sure to find out for you, Dawn."

"When's this big date taking place?"

"Saturday night."

"Thank goodness it's not on Friday. We have a big game on Saturday. I wouldn't want our keeper to be defending our goal with rose-tinted glasses on. You wouldn't be able to see the ball coming."

"I would never let the mere inkling of a love life interfere with a big game for the Darlings." Amelia made a fist. "The team before everything."

"Speaking of. Have you made any progress on your 40+ team?"

"None whatsoever," Amelia admitted.

"Maybe it's time for us to quit soccer and join Cindy's choir." Dawn sounded dead serious.

"I think we have a few more good years in us and, who knows, by then a 40+ league might have spontaneously come into existence. We can't be the only female players getting older and feeling a bit out of place on our current teams, surrounded by youngsters who are much better on the ball than we ever were."

"Correction. *You* feel out of place. I've never had that feeling."

"Lucky you, but it's not because you haven't felt it that you won't in the future."

"Have you considered the option of a mixed team?"

"You mean with… men?"

"Well, I wasn't referring to animals. I adore my pups, but Samson and Delilah have only ever ripped a football to shreds. I wouldn't count on them being any good at passing."

Amelia laughed. Not for one split second had she considered a mixed team. "I don't want to play on a team with a bunch of middle-aged men."

"Even if it meant no longer playing at all?"

"Fair point."

"They don't have to be straight men, you know. Lots of gays play soccer. We should be able to find some."

"I will need to think about that." Amelia didn't believe too many gay men over forty would be eager to join her brand-new team, but it was worth considering. "I've been thinking about something else." After discussing it with Jill, maybe she should broach the subject with her best friend. "I'm not sure I want to go back to the pharmaceutical industry."

Dawn drew up her eyebrows. "Yeah. I guess I can see that. They did squeeze you dry." She eyed her empty wine glass. "Have you thought about what you might do instead?"

"Yes, but I haven't really found anything that might interest me."

"As a teacher, I can sing the praises of my noble profession. I can also tell you quite a few horror stories, of course." Dawn chuckled. "And you have to think of those poor, impressionable teenagers. It's such a tender age, you know, and to be faced with you as their science teacher might make it hard for them to focus on chemistry. It would be good for the sciences in general, though. A revamp is in order. What better way to accomplish that than a hot new teacher!"

"Don't be silly."

"You know, sometimes I think that when you look in the mirror you don't see the same as what I, or Sophia, or your former therapist, see. You are one hot goalkeeper, Melly."

"Oh, please." Amelia had never been able to take a compliment about her looks. What was there to be proud of, anyway? She wasn't responsible for the shape of her face or the color of her eyes. It was all just genetics. And sure, maybe she'd been quite lucky in that department—but she hadn't lucked out in others, so it all evened itself out in the end.

"Seriously," Dawn said. "After *two* sessions with your therapist, the poor woman had to confess to having a crush on you. That sort of thing just doesn't happen to most people. You've always had a string of admirers, but most of the time, you don't even realize it." Dawn tapped her finger against her chin. "I think that's actually one of the things that drew me to Sophia. She wasn't afraid to just go for it with you, despite this… intimidating quality you have."

"Intimidating quality? What are you talking about?"

"I know you're sensitive about this, and I know you've always preferred to hide inside that white lab coat of yours, protected by your nerdy ways, but you're a hot piece of ass. You are, by far, the most beautiful woman I've met in my life."

"Are you messing with me? Is this some sort of hidden camera thing?" Amelia leaned in Dawn's direction. "What about Cindy?"

"Cindy is utterly adorable and I love her to bits," Dawn said in her history-teacher tone of voice. "But put you next to Cindy and ask a thousand random strangers who is the prettier woman and 999 of them will pick you. You have that kind of face. Very symmetrical and pleasing to the eye. Add to that your mysterious smile and that super low voice of yours. No one else stands a chance." Dawn shrugged. "That's why it's so quote-unquote safe for me to have a crush on Sophia. I pale in comparison to you. She barely notices me when you're around."

"You aren't confessing some long-held secret to me, are you?" Amelia had to ask.

"I've always been quite immune to your beauty. I'm into a different style of woman. A little less polished. A bit more…"

"A bit more what?" This conversation was getting beyond ridiculous, yet Amelia was keen to find out what else Dawn thought about her.

"You're my best friend and I love you, but… you're a person with her head in the clouds. You're not very practical or… even realistic at times. Yes, you love hard science, but sometimes it's like your job is a crutch to you, or a thick, firm wall to hide behind."

Amelia swallowed hard. "W—what do you mean? I never knew you thought these things about me."

"Your burnout has made me think about you and how you are. How you got to be so burned out and beat down and depressed. I wasn't going to tell you while you were still in the darkest depths of it. In fact, I hadn't really planned on telling you today, or ever, for that matter. But now I have, so there you go."

"What am I not realistic about?" Amelia's heart sank all the way into her stomach.

Dawn blew some air from her puffed-up cheeks. "Gosh, I'm so not prepared for this."

"Neither am I, so..."

Dawn took a breath. "On the one hand, you are this gorgeous woman. I'm serious. You could have anyone you wanted, but that has never seemed to interest you. The women you have chosen to date have always been so... utterly unserious about you. I can only guess that's how you wanted it. On the other hand, for the past twenty years, you have held yourself to an impossible professional standard. Always being the first to arrive at the lab and the last to leave. Always pushing harder. Always reaching for some form of perfection that doesn't exist. It's no wonder you crashed, Amelia. It might be hard for you to hear, but the only direction left for you to go was all the way down."

This was not how Amelia and Dawn usually communicated. Dawn had always been there to lend an ear and offer support, but she'd never been this direct. Did she fancy herself as Amelia's new therapist now?

"Jesus," Amelia said, because she didn't know what else to say. A part of her wanted to go on the defensive—because she did feel under attack—but this was Dawn. If Dawn was speaking to her like this, she must have a damn good reason for it.

"I hope you know I always mean well with you," Dawn said. "I love you like family, Melly. You're my son's godmother for a reason. You know I don't take things like that lightly."

"I can be practical if I have to be," Amelia muttered under her breath.

This made Dawn snicker. "Like that time you tried to hang your new curtains and ended up with a twisted ankle and a black-and-blue knee?"

"And a very bruised ego," Amelia added.

"Hey." Dawn's voice had lowered to a whisper. "I can tell you're doing better and I'm so pleased about that." She put her hand on the table between them, palm upward. Amelia reached for it. "It's good to have a little bit more of my best friend back. I've missed you."

"Is that why you went and had the hots for a woman more than ten years younger than you? Because you were missing me?" Amelia was still processing what Dawn had said about her, so it was easier to refocus the conversation on Dawn's crush on Sophia.

Dawn grinned. "That's right. It's all your fault."

"So you think I'm gorgeous, huh." Amelia was joking. She never thought of herself in those terms. She was yet to meet the first woman who did.

"It's the only reason I've put up with you for so long. Your dazzling beauty." Dawn squeezed her hand.

"I do know that I've taken my work much too seriously for far too long. That perfectionist streak was something I was hoping to work on with my therapist."

"I do hope the new one you're going to see is either a gay man," Dawn said, "or a woman as straight as a broomstick."

Chapter Twenty-Three

JILL DABBED a few drops of perfume behind her ears. For the umpteenth time, she ran a hand through her hair. She straightened her blouse, smiled at her reflection in the mirror, looked away, and inspected her appearance again, before finally leaving the house.

She was meeting Amelia at a restaurant called Sixth Sense. It was only a few blocks away so Jill opted to walk.

Being a self-confessed restaurant snob, Amelia had picked the venue for their first official date. *A date.* Jill could hardly believe it, yet there she was, getting closer to the venue for said date, with every step she took.

Since the evening of the kiss, they had only exchanged a few text messages, but Amelia's eagerness easily shone through the words on the screen. Or maybe that was just wishful thinking on Jill's part. Maybe Amelia was just feeling guilty about breaking that glass that cut Jill's hand. She glanced at the small bandage. In a few days, she would have forgotten all about it. But she would never forget how that tiny shard of glass had gotten lodged into her flesh in the first place.

When she reached the restaurant, Amelia was already there. Jill's heart did a double-take when she saw her at the table. Amelia's hair was loose and a little wild. Jill wondered if it was how her hair naturally fell or if Amelia had to spend hours to get it to do that. Either way, it looked silky and magnificent and very inviting for Jill to run her hands through—which she had done the other night and it hadn't been a disappointing sensation at all.

When she noticed Jill, Amelia sent her the most devastating smile. Jill could pontificate to Vic about seeing Amelia's strength behind her struggles all she wanted, but, if she was being completely honest, it had been nothing but Amelia's striking beauty—and her voice—that had done her in from the get-go. Those brown almond-shaped eyes. The tilt of her lips when she grinned. Every line on her face, even the ones that deepened with age, only designed to make her face more appealing.

Amelia rose when Jill reached the table and, while gently pressing a hand to Jill's arm, kissed her on the cheek. She smelled flowery and sultry at the same time. Jill's mouth settled into a smile she probably wouldn't be able to wipe off her face for the rest of the night.

"Great to see you," Amelia said. "How's the hand?"

"Absolutely fine. Must have been the excellent first aid skills."

Amelia gave her what seemed to be an eye roll, but Jill wasn't sure. "For such a world-class goalkeeper, I can be surprisingly clumsy."

"I've never seen you in action, so I'll have to take your word for that."

A server stopped by with menus. Jill took the opportunity to glance around the restaurant. So far, she'd only had eyes for Amelia. Despite the restaurant's obvious swankiness, with plenty of little details in the decor that warranted further investigation, Jill couldn't pull her gaze away from Amelia for more than a few seconds. She tried studying the menu next, but she encountered the same issue. When the server came to take their order, she'd just ask him for today's special.

Amelia had unearthed a pair of reading glasses from her bag. Lips pursed, she managed an admirable job of studying what was on offer.

It was the first time Jill had seen her with a pair of glasses. It gave her a slightly stern, sexy scientist look, which made Jill feel even hotter under the collar than she already was.

"Everything okay?" Amelia glanced at her from over the rim of her glasses.

"I've never seen you with glasses on." For heaven's sake. Could Jill sound any more like an adolescent on a first date?

"I need them for reading." Amelia took them off. "Old age isn't kind to any of us."

Jill snickered. First of all, because Amelia was only forty-five. And secondly, because, glasses or not, she looked scrumptious all the time. She even looked hot in her soccer kit—as far as Jill had been able to see on the Darlinghurst Darlings' website, although she had no doubt that Amelia did the kit justice in real life as well.

The server came by again to ask if they wanted to order drinks. He recommended their house cocktail of Champagne and blackberry liqueur and Jill happily went with that. After a few moments of hesitation, so did Amelia.

"If I wanted to see you in action." Thinking of Amelia in her soccer kit had given Jill a bold idea. "Would that be possible?"

"Depends what action you have in mind." Amelia's voice was so sultry, Jill had to take a moment to let the flirty banter wash over her.

"Soccer. What else?"

"Ah, right. I'm glad we're on the same page. All I talk about is soccer, so..." With a smile, Amelia put the menu to the side. "You can see the Darlinghurst Darlings in action every other Saturday at 10AM at the Darlinghurst sports ground."

"You had a game this morning?"

Amelia nodded, a beaming smile appearing on her face. "We won. Dawn was on it. She scored twice. Maybe because Sophia was the one who gave her the assists. They're starting to play really well together." Her shapely eyebrows inched toward each other as she frowned. "I hope they haven't been practicing after hours."

"Even if they have, it's not necessarily something for you to worry about," Jill offered.

Amelia stared at her in disbelief. "Of course it is. I don't want Dawn and Cindy to split up."

"I see how you would make that leap, and sure, maybe there's a small possibility of that actually being the result of two women on the same soccer team practicing together, but even if it were, it still wouldn't be your responsibility. It's not your job to stop it."

"Who else is going to talk some sense into Dawn?"

"*Dawn.* She's the one responsible for her actions. She's the one making the decisions. It's not something you have much control over."

"Seeing as this is decidedly not a therapy session, could you summarize your conclusion, please? Just so I don't accidentally misinterpret it." There was a hint of bite to Amelia's tone.

Jill was grateful for their cocktails arriving. In daily life, it was hard enough to shake off her therapist mentality, but with a former client, no matter how much she liked her on a personal level, it was even harder.

After the server had taken their food order, she said, "I'm

sorry." She lifted her glass. "I slipped into inadvertent shrink mode there for a second. Professional hazard. I'll pay more attention to it from now on." Amelia's smile helped deflate her worries. "It's been a while since I've been on a date. Shall we start again?"

"Sure." They tasted their cocktails. "Not bad," Amelia said.

Jill concurred.

"Now that we're on the subject of Dawn," Amelia continued, "the other night, she… well, let's just say she told me a few harsh truths."

"She did?" Jill canted her head.

A darkness crossed Amelia's face. "She said some things I wasn't expecting. Things that have made me even more nervous about this date than I already was."

"Why don't we start by admitting that we're both nervous then." Jill drank from her cocktail again. The second sip was even better than the first. "What did Dawn say?"

Amelia twirled her glass between her fingers. "I guess what it came down to…" She heaved a small sigh. "That I've always had pretty terrible taste in women, but also that I'm too much of a perfectionist. Both things, according to Dawn, have contributed to my burnout." Amelia shot her a furtive glance. "Maybe she's right."

"You're not sure?" It was really hard for Jill not to sound like a therapist. If they had been in session, she would follow up a statement like that with a couple of well-aimed questions, but she'd already sounded so therapeutic earlier. She took another sip instead.

"It was more hearing those things from Dawn's mouth that shocked me. Of course, I know I haven't had much of a love life. I know I've put way too much of my energy into my work without getting enough back for it. But I always had the time. Because I've never been in a relationship that felt worthy of coming before my job. One thing has fed into the other. I can see that."

To hell with it, Jill thought. She was very keen to figure out why Amelia had never invested her time in a long-term relationship and there simply was no viable way to ask that didn't sound like a therapist. "Do you know why you've never had much of a love life?"

"According to Dawn it's because the women I fall for don't take me seriously." Amelia shrugged.

"Did you take them seriously?"

Amelia huffed out some air. "Probably not seriously enough. It's hard to build something stable when you have to cancel dates all the time because you're working late. I've always seen it as a matter of priorities. I've always put work first. And if I did feel… frisky, it was never hard for me to find someone to spend some time with."

Jill could easily imagine that.

"Not every person on this planet," Amelia continued, "grows up dreaming of a fairy-tale wedding. I always knew I was different. Not just because I'm gay. I know this is going to sound silly, but… I guess I've always been in love with science more." She made a funny, self-deprecating motion with her eyebrows. "The women I've ended up with, they never seemed very interested in science. I know it's not for everyone, but I like to discuss string theory and quantum physics over dinner. What can I say?" Luckily, she followed up with a smile that said—Jill hoped—no such thing would be required tonight.

"But then you fell out of love with science—or at least with your current work circumstances."

Amelia nodded. "Cue the burnout, followed by therapy, followed by being on a date with my ex-therapist, followed by… I don't know yet. How's that for cause and consequence, though?" She chuckled heartily.

Jill laughed with her. From the corner of her eye, she noticed the server bringing over their starters. That was the big difference between a dinner date and a therapy session—natural breaks. The chance to start the conversation again and go into a completely new direction. There was no preferred outcome as a goal for tonight—at least not when it came to Amelia's mental health, because she was no longer her client. To think Jill had wanted to keep her on as long as possible. However, letting her go, although highly embarrassing at the time, had led to this.

"Hm, this is so good." Amelia closed her eyes as she tasted her dish. "I'm so glad we came here. I've been wanting to try it out for ages but I guess I was waiting for a special occasion."

"I'm very pleased to be your special occasion." While the food was excellent, being in Amelia's company overwhelmed any other sensation.

Amelia gave a slight shake of the head. "I can't believe we're talking about me again. Over to you, Jill. How was your week?"

"Rather interesting." She held up her hand. "I cut myself on some glass."

"How did you manage that?" Amelia's smile turned to high beam.

"It was an accident—I hope. Come to think of it, I should check with the other party involved."

"I can only hope it hasn't rendered you incapable of performing certain tasks." Amelia emitted a low chuckle.

Another hot flash coursed through Jill. She felt it flare up her cheeks. She was blushing like a teen in heat. *Great.* It didn't matter because the reason for her skin's betrayal of her desires was Amelia's flirting. "My job isn't very hands-on," Jill said.

"Have you…"—Amelia's fork stopped halfway between

her plate and her delicious mouth—"dated anyone since you broke up with Rasmus?"

"No." Jill paused. "I felt like some time on my own was required after such a long relationship."

Amelia nodded as though she understood. "Not even a booty call?"

Jill nearly spat out the forkful of rice she'd just put into her mouth.

"I don't think that's what the kids call it these days," Amelia said matter-of-factly. "But I don't bother trying to keep up with the lingo of my younger teammates." Her lips spread into a smile now.

Jill had regained her composure. "No, not even a booty call," she confirmed. Something Amelia had said earlier had stuck in her mind. "You?"

"Me what?" Amelia asked, as though she wasn't the one who had instigated their shift in conversation.

But if Jill had one super-advanced skill, it was to direct a question right back at the person sitting across from her with zero qualms, even on a date. "You said earlier that you never have trouble finding someone 'to spend time with'. That was your way of referring to a booty call, I assume."

Amelia put her fork down and regarded Jill intently, but she didn't say anything.

"What?" Jill asked because the prolonged silence was making her feel a touch uncomfortable.

"Another reason as to why I like you so much just hit me."

Warmth spread through Jill's chest. She waited for Amelia to continue.

"You're the opposite of coy," Amelia said. "You're not afraid to ask a difficult or potentially embarrassing question."

Part of the job, Jill thought, but didn't think it opportune to mention under the circumstances. "Thank you," she said.

"Was that the perfect example of an embarrassing question?"

Amelia chuckled. "You're also very good at replying to a question with another question."

Jill shrugged, although she was feeling anything but nonchalant. "Speaking of… Are you going to answer my previous question at all?"

Amelia huffed out some air. "I haven't really been in the mood for any booty calls lately."

Jill nodded. It was inevitable that the conversation would always come back to Amelia's burnout. "Does that imply that if you had been, all you would have to do is pick up your phone and call someone?"

"Wow. You've really been out of the game for a long time. *Call* someone?" She shook her head. "That's very last century." Amelia's eyes sparkled. She obviously found a lot of glee in needling Jill.

Jill didn't mind one bit. It was amazing to witness Amelia come alive like that. And while Jill had, indeed, been out of the game for a long time, she was still very much aware that, in a situation like this, teasing equaled flirting.

"Okay." Jill drank some water—her head was swimming already, and not just from that house cocktail. "Let's reset, shall we."

Amelia smiled gently. "Let's take it as agreed that neither one of us has been very active for a while." She lifted her glass. "To abstinence."

"There's a first." Jill clinked her glass against Amelia's, although not having had any sex for such a long time was the last thing she wanted to toast to while looking into Amelia's deep-brown eyes.

Chapter Twenty-Four

"I UNDERSTAND THE SCIENCE OF IT," Amelia said. "The relentless cortisol cycle of modern-day life. It's biochemistry." Amelia didn't just like Jill because she could be very straightforward in a non-threatening way, she also very much liked the fact that she was a doctor—that she had the knowledge that kept Amelia from having to explain certain things. "I used to be able to break that cycle by playing soccer and spending time with my friends, until that stopped being enough."

Jill didn't interrupt her. Amelia supposed being a therapist made her the best listener in all of Sydney, possibly Australia. Another attribute to admire in Jill, who also had the most mesmerizing, perpetually half-lidded eyes.

"And it's so insidious. I never even noticed until it was too late and for that..." Very much aware that she was dominating the conversation, Amelia paused. Jill gave her a gentle, encouraging nod. "For that I blame capitalism. It just sucks you dry. When you really start thinking what capitalism has done to our humanity, it's simply mind-boggling." She brought a hand to her chest. "Not just to me, with my burnout, but to so many people in so many forms. The exploitation. The non-stop pursuit of profit at the expense of the environment. But also to our brain." Amelia shook her head. "They don't teach you any of that in school. At least they didn't in my day."

"Some things can't be taught in school," Jill said. "Some things are only learned by living life."

The server stopped by to retrieve their empty plates.

"Do you think me suffering from burnout is life teaching me a lesson?" Amelia asked after the server had gone.

"That's not what I was implying."

"I know, but—" Amelia took a breath. "God, I'm doing it again. I feel like we need a safe word."

"For what?" Jill skimmed her fingertip over the rim of her glass. The gesture made Amelia feel something she couldn't identify.

"For me banging on and on about myself and all my insecurities."

"That's not how I see it. It's all right to be vulnerable, Amelia. If anything, I'm flattered you can still talk to me about this outside my office."

"I made an appointment with Dr. Scarpa," Amelia said, by way of apology. "She can start seeing me in two weeks."

"I know the lines are blurred between us," Jill said. "While I'm no longer your therapist, that doesn't mean you can't talk to me and it certainly doesn't mean that I won't help where I can. I'm here for you."

What Amelia liked about Jill most of all was her abundant kindness. "Thank you." If they hadn't been in a restaurant, Amelia would have jumped out of her chair and kissed Jill there and then.

The server dropped by with the dessert menu. Amelia only pretended to glance at it. She knew what she wanted for dessert and it wasn't to be found on that menu. She waited for Jill to put hers down.

"How about," Amelia offered, "we go for a walk instead?" Amelia surprised herself by being so forward, but she guessed that was the result of Jill being so open about how smitten she was with her. It left far less room for self-doubt.

"A walk it is." Jill agreed, a grin plastered across her face.

Maybe Dawn had been right. Maybe Amelia had never paid the right kind of attention to women who would take her seriously—to women like Jill. Maybe it was time she started focusing on that part of her life, despite not feeling ready for it yet. But what would being ready actually feel like? She was on a dream date with a dream woman who had all the right feelings for her. Even if Amelia didn't feel 100% ready, surely the circumstances were pushing her toward it.

After an awkward few minutes during which Jill insisted on paying—"No is simply not an option"—and Amelia vowed that, in that case, she would pay next time, they stood outside the restaurant.

"We've been to your place," Jill said. "How about a walk to mine for a nightcap?"

As soon as they started walking, Amelia hooked her arm into Jill's. There was a slight chill in the air and Amelia had to stop herself from throwing her arm all the way around Jill to make sure she was warm enough.

"I might have mentioned that I'm a footballer," Amelia said. "How do you relax after work?"

"Books and wine," Jill said without missing a beat. "I belong to a book club called 'Reading between the wines'."

"Do you actually read the books or just drink the wine?" Amelia reveled in the warmth of Jill's body next to hers, in walking in step with another woman.

"Truth be told, due to the aforementioned capitalism, because most of us are always too busy doing something else, our little club hasn't gotten together in months. I don't have to tell you how it goes." Jill stilled. "I always read the books, though. But I often 'read between the wines' on my own." She chuckled. "I also love movies. And art. And I keep an eye on what's on at Sydney Opera House."

"Sounds very highbrow." Amelia held onto Jill's arm a little tighter as she guided them toward her house.

"Maybe that's what it sounds like, but I actually despise arty-farty-ness for the sake of it. If it doesn't make sense to me one way or another, I'm out."

"What are you saying? That you're more of a multiplex woman than an arthouse cinema one?"

"God no." Jill leaned into her a little. "Maybe I am a touch arty-farty, depending on the observer. To myself, I'm not."

They turned a corner.

"I just like good entertainment. I like to be moved. Maybe learn something about the human spirit along the way. That's it. My standards aren't so high, are they?"

"From my point of view, your standards are impeccable." Amelia glanced sideways and looked straight into Jill's eyes.

"You would say that."

"Actually, I wouldn't." Amelia slowed their step. "When you've been where I've been mentally, your self-esteem really takes a hit. But your interest in me has done me the world of good."

"I'm glad that excruciating moment in therapy was good for something," Jill said.

"I can imagine it was difficult for you, but I really admire you for telling me. That's a hard thing to do. I don't think I could have done that."

"I had no choice," Jill said. "I can't put my own interests before the client's."

"But still."

"But still," Jill repeated, and steered them toward a small town house. She unlocked the door and ushered Amelia in. "Here we are." She switched on the lights.

"Wow." Amelia didn't know where to look first. "You weren't kidding about being into art." A number of paintings covered the walls, and a built-in bookcase that stretched all the way to the ceiling, filled to the brim. "And about reading." On instinct, Amelia walked to the bookcase. Propped against a few book spines, she spotted an invitation to an art show opening.

Jill picked up the invite. "Maybe you could come with me?" She arched up her eyebrows. "My favorite gallery. It's in Potts Point." She pointed at a painting on the opposite wall. "I got that one there and"—she nodded in the direction of a painting above the chimney—"that one as well. I know the owners."

"Did you just ask me out on another date? Before this one has even ended?" Amelia held out her hand for the invitation. "When is it?"

"Thursday next week." Jill gave her the glossy white card with red and blue splotches of paint embossed in it.

"I have soccer practice on Thursdays." Amelia studied the invitation. The Griffith-Porter gallery, it said.

"Too bad." Jill tilted her head.

"I have been known to skip practice on occasion the past couple of months, but never to be arty-farty with a beautiful woman." She beamed Jill a smile.

"What's the penalty for missing practice? Being benched?" Jill took a step closer. "Because I was planning to come and watch you play."

"The Darlinghurst Darlings don't have a spare goalkeeper so my position's pretty safe." Amelia put the invitation back on the bookshelf. Heat fizzled underneath her skin. She wanted the nightcap Jill had offered to mainly consist of kissing and she was getting the impression Jill might be on the same page about that.

"I'll be there," Jill whispered.

"I've had a very lovely time with you tonight." Gingerly, Amelia lifted up Jill's injured hand. "Do you need me to change that bandage?"

Jill shook her head. "I would like you to do something else for me, though."

"Anything." Amelia gazed into Jill's eyes.

"Come here." Jill tugged her closer. "And kiss me."

Butterflies flapped their tiny wings in Amelia's stomach. She stepped closer to Jill, and cupped her cheeks with her hands. What a strange sensation to feel so numb, so utterly uninterested in anything, to have her brain suffused by nothing but anxiety and thought loops that got her nowhere and then rise from near-nothingness to this. This surge in her blood. This energy buzzing through her skin. To face this glorious, kind woman waiting to be kissed by her. Jill, who saw something in Amelia that she believed she had lost, that was buried under layers of disillusion and the aftereffects of the hormonal imbalance that had knocked Amelia so off course.

What an odd time to fall in love.

When Amelia pressed her lips gently against Jill's, it wasn't just the delicious memory of the previous time they had done this that washed over her. The soft meeting of their lips was a gesture filled with hope, with a glimpse of how life could be different again. This time around, after the lovely evening they'd just had, there was no sign of glaring red lights or annoying klaxons going off in her brain. There was just the tenderness of Jill's lips, and how she opened them, to welcome Amelia's tongue.

The intimacy of that took Amelia to a whole new level of knowing that, yes, this was what she had missed. Only, she'd had no real way of knowing before. Because she'd never kissed a woman like Jill before. Well, she'd never had a therapist before—but that wasn't the biggest distinguishing factor here.

Maybe Amelia had met women like Jill, but if she had, she'd been too preoccupied with other things to notice. The reason why she'd never been in a long-term relationship wasn't so much the women she had ended up with before—the ones Dawn claimed weren't serious enough about her—it was Amelia subconsciously picking them because of their aloofness, their obvious desire to remain unattached—all the things Amelia saw mirrored in them because that was how she presented herself.

Jill pressed herself against Amelia's body, the swell of her breasts easily noticeable. While their tongues continued to explore each other's mouths, Amelia's legs went a little limp. A hardness that had snuck into her muscles months ago, gave way to something a lot softer, a lot more malleable, a lot more receptive to this utterly divine sensation of kissing a woman without qualms. Without projecting into the future and how badly this could possibly end. Without expectations. It was just a kiss. A coming together of two women who really fancied each other—who were falling in love with each other. Not a single cell in Amelia's body wanted to shut this down.

Jill ran a hand along Amelia's side and despite her touch being featherlight, it sent sparks all the way down between Amelia's legs, to that deep spot that had seemed so dead all this time. She leaned into Jill's touch, letting her know she wanted more of that, more of her. Jill obliged. She dug her fingertips into Amelia's flesh a little deeper, a little more intentionally.

So Jill wanted more as well—not that Amelia ever had many doubts about that. Maybe that was what had brought her here, to kissing Jill against her massive bookshelf and enjoying every single second of it. Jill's honesty and how she said, earlier, that she'd had no choice but to tell Amelia. As if curbing her emerging feelings for Amelia was simply not an option. That had been the spark and now here she was—so much further than she'd imagined herself to be.

They broke apart, coming up for air, their lips eager for more but in need of a break. Jill looked at Amelia, her glance searching—maybe for any signs of the distress Amelia had displayed the first time they'd kissed.

"Are you okay with this?" Jill asked.

"Fuck yeah." Amelia draped her arms around Jill's neck.

"It's not too much?"

"The opposite." Amelia leaned in again, but instead of finding Jill's lips with hers, she found her ear, and whispered, "Thank you for giving me this."

Chapter Twenty-Five

AT LAST, Jill thought. The kiss she'd been hoping for, waiting for. The kiss she could allow, and the kiss Amelia didn't need to pull away from. Even though they'd kissed before, it still felt like this was their first proper kiss.

How Amelia had been sitting at the restaurant when Jill had arrived—waiting for her. How Amelia had whispered in her ear, her voice even lower than usual, her lips moving against Jill's skin as she spoke. It all still felt like a dream. To think it had all begun so awkwardly. But Amelia was here, in Jill's house. What had started as a sweet and gentle kiss, a tentative exploration, was quickly turning into something much more urgent.

Jill's fingers tightened as the urgency manifested itself. She seemed incapable of a restrained caress. All her fingers wanted to do was tug at Amelia's clothes so Jill could see even more of her. So they could come even closer.

Even though it went against her every instinct, Jill managed to control herself. She had to. Overwhelming desire was never an excuse for anything. Amelia had to lead the charge. Jill had to remain receptive to her cues, to what her body signaled when her voice couldn't form the words. Although, right now, all Amelia's body language conveyed was how much she wanted Jill. One of her hands roamed through Jill's hair while the other held Jill close. Not an inch of space was left between their bodies.

Amelia's lips drifted to Jill's cheek, her jaw, and down to her neck. Jill feared that the divine sensations Amelia elicited inside her might prevent her from exercising the one percent of alertness she had left.

Amelia's body swiveled and she pushed Jill against the bookcase so that the shelves pressed into her back.

Even if this was all Amelia could ever give her, it would be enough. But no, that was absolute nonsense. Jill wanted so much more. She wanted her hands all over Amelia. She wanted her out of those clothes, no matter how elegant they looked on her. She wanted Amelia in her bed, as ready and hot for Jill as she was for her. Because Jill was more than ready. The stubborn pulse that ran through her told her so. Her entire being throbbed with desire for Amelia. For more of her kisses, more of her touch. For her ultimate surrender.

But even as Jill stood with her back against the bookshelf with Amelia all over her, her hair silky against her cheeks, her lips like the smoothest velvet on her neck, deep down, Jill knew that more patience would be required. That Amelia was still vulnerable and that a bout of kissing, no matter how passionate, would not magically make her ready to open herself up completely to another human being. Not after what she'd been through. Burgeoning romance could have a touch of magic to it—how else to explain how two people could find each other as they had and lose themselves in each other like this mere weeks after? But it wasn't magic in itself.

Amelia's hand slid down from Jill's hair to her shoulder, inching ever lower. Jill felt its gentle push against the side of her breast. Her nipple reacted by straining hard against the inside of her bra. Maybe Jill should have dealt with this pent-up friskiness before she left for this date, although it wouldn't have made a difference. Her body stood no chance against Amelia's allure, no matter how much sexual energy Jill might have spent beforehand. Amelia was like a hurricane of the most exquisite sultriness, with her moody glance and her broody voice and those lips, oh those lips. To feel them on her skin with such abundance was more than enough to make Jill's clit rise to attention as much as her nipples.

If Jill was going to check in with Amelia at all before this spiraled totally out of control, she had to do so now. A few more minutes of this and Jill would no longer be able to account for her actions. Not that she would ever cross any of Amelia's boundaries willingly, but she wanted to make sure that Amelia wasn't rushing into something she might later regret—that she wasn't pushing past a line she wasn't ready to cross. That she'd suffered a burnout meant that she might have a history of not always recognizing her own boundaries. Being Amelia's former therapist didn't release Jill from the duty to ensure Amelia was 100% okay with where this was going—no matter how much she wanted her.

"Hey," Jill whispered. "Let's take a second." She ran a hand through her hair while she let Amelia compose herself.

"Are you okay?" Amelia asked.

"Can we sit? Maybe have that nightcap?" Jill made sure the smile she shot Amelia was the warmest she could muster.

"Sure." Amelia straightened her posture.

"What can I get you?" Jill asked.

"Just some water is fine." Amelia strode to the couch. "I forgot that kissing is a thirsty business."

Jill fetched a bottle of water and two glasses from the kitchen. She took the opportunity to think about what she would say. It was really hard not to sound like a therapist when that was what you were. But this was a delicate moment. Apart from that, Jill also had the incessant throbbing between her legs to deal with.

When she walked back into the living room, Amelia was standing next to the sideboard where Jill kept a picture of her and Rasmus.

"Is this your ex?" Amelia asked.

Jill nodded.

"He couldn't look more Swedish if he tried."

While Jill waited for Amelia to join her on the couch, she poured them a glass of water.

"Did you live here with him?" Amelia seemed to study the picture in detail.

"No. I moved here not long after we broke up. I didn't want to stay in the house where we lived together. Fresh start and all that."

Amelia smoothed a wrinkle out of her blouse, cleared her throat, and then, finally, came to sit next to Jill. She took a sip of water.

"Did I come on too strong?" she asked, after she put her glass back down.

"Heavens, no." All Jill wanted to do was pull Amelia close and kiss her again. "I just wouldn't be able to forgive myself if we rushed into this… into something we're not ready for. With what I know about you, I need to be certain this is what you really want."

Amelia nodded. "I get it. And I appreciate that."

"Besides, we have time." Jill reached out her hand. Amelia took it in hers.

"You're so considerate. It's quite rare, in my experience." Amelia traced a fingertip over the lines in Jill's palm.

"It's not only consideration for your feelings. I've been single for almost a year and while it's very enticing to just lose myself in this avalanche of feelings I have for you, I'm not without trepidation. On the one hand, it's hard to shake that you were in my care. And then there's the tiny fact that I haven't been with a woman in a very long time."

"Are you nervous?" Amelia lifted Jill's hand and planted a kiss on the heel of her palm.

Oh, goodness. Yes, Jill was nervous, but she was also extremely aroused. "A bit."

"Because of how long it's been for you or because of what I told you in therapy?"

"Both."

"Let me assure you that when we were kissing earlier, I felt very in touch with my body." Amelia painted on a slightly wicked grin. "I felt alive. I felt like… being with you was all that mattered."

Jill could only smile.

"Maybe…" Amelia shuffled a little closer. "You worry about me a little too much."

"I can't help it."

"At least I know you're not just after my body." Amelia followed up with a chuckle.

"It's been so crazy, this whole thing." Jill wrapped her fingers around Amelia's knee. "I knew I was in some sort of trouble from the minute you walked into my office. That has honestly never happened to me before. It was like this instant attraction that I didn't know what to do with. A part of me still believes that me sitting here with you right now, in my house, having this conversation about where to go next, is fundamentally wrong. I've been in this job for a long time and some things get drilled into you. You learn how to keep your distance, how to keep that wall intact. I've never had any trouble with that, until you came along. Part of me can't help but see that in a pretty bad light." Like a blatant failure, Jill added in her head.

"Life's hardly ever as clear-cut as we'd like it to be." Amelia covered Jill's hand with hers. "I'm pretty sure I should be focusing on me right now, on my recovery and on getting better, yet you're all I think about." She shrugged. "But I've chosen not to obsess about that. Because I do have that choice. And yes, last week, when we kissed in your office, I couldn't deal with it. But today, I can. Today, I'm ready, although I don't know what 'ready' actually means in this context." Amelia locked her gaze on Jill's. "When we kiss now, it takes away all the doubt instead of adding to it." She huffed out some air. "What I'm trying to say, in my very own convoluted way, is that I appreciate your concern for me, I really do, but I can assert myself. I think you know that I can. I'll worry about me. You worry about you."

"So beautiful and so smart. How's it even possible?" Jill scooted a little closer to Amelia.

"You only have to look in the mirror to know all about that." Amelia smiled. "Too corny?"

"Hell no."

"But, um…" Amelia's smile faded. "All of that being said, I don't think I should stay tonight. I mean, I want to. I want you, but, you're right, we have time. We don't have to rush."

Relief and disappointment warred within Jill, although she knew that Amelia was making perfect sense. She nodded. "Of course."

"As much as I enjoy kissing you, I also really enjoy talking to you," Amelia said. "Maybe we can do some more of that."

"As long as we start with kissing." Lips already pursed, Jill leaned in.

Chapter Twenty-Six

The candles were lit. A soothing playlist hummed in the background. The tub was almost full. Amelia checked the temperature. Perfect. Like most people who suffered a burnout, Amelia had gone down a search engine rabbit hole to unearth the secret to making herself feel better. She'd soon been bombarded with ads promoting this kind of advanced mindfulness slash yoga slash relaxation exercise and that kind of magic potion to be applied to her temples twice each day to put her mind at ease, all of which had been easy enough for Amelia to ignore because she wasn't going to fall down the trap of consumerism even more. She couldn't rail against the fallacies of capitalism while spending money earned doing a job that had, ultimately, left her so empty and disillusioned. It just didn't fly.

What she could do was fill her previously hardly used bathtub—decades of playing soccer and sharing locker rooms had made her the world's quickest showerer—and let the hot water calm her frayed nerves.

Today, she could immerse herself in the hot water while thinking of Jill. Thoughtful, sweet Jill. The more she considered Jill, the more Amelia was convinced she'd never met anyone like her. Because, last night, Amelia would have gone all the way. When she'd kissed Jill, it felt as though a switch in her head had been flipped. No more apprehension. No more endless thought loops. No more fear of opening herself up like that. She had just wanted Jill—Jill who wanted Amelia so much, it was noticeable in her smallest gestures. Yet Jill had pressed the pause button. She had given Amelia more time—time that Amelia, in that heated moment, hadn't even known she needed.

Amelia turned off the faucet and lowered herself slowly into the tub. The water was so hot, she had to introduce her skin to it inch by inch. With a controlled motion, she lay back, letting the hot water engulf all of her except her face, and waited for the moment of release in her shoulders. For that moment when the heat of the water worked its way into her muscles and relaxed her completely. Ah, there it was.

The heat spread through her entire body, the water cleansing her from the inside as well as the outside. Her too-tight muscles relaxed. Her body surrendered to the water, her limbs carried by it, her skin caressed by it. No ninety-nine-dollar gadget could ever make her feel like this. Baths against burnouts. Amelia believed doctors should prescribe this as part of the cure.

Instead of drying herself when she stepped out of the tub, Amelia put a large towel on her bed and lay on top of it until she had cooled down. Mellow from the hot water, with her mind, as if by magic, as relaxed as her body, Amelia sank into the softness of the towel, and simply lay there. No deep thoughts were required. No specific way of breathing was recommended. All she had to do was just lie there and let her body come to a normal human temperature again.

Instantly, her mind was saturated with thoughts of Jill. Jill, who had told her last night that she felt as if she'd been out of her depth as soon as Amelia had sat opposite her. How about that?

It made Amelia wonder when she had first developed feelings for Jill. Was it when Jill had been so delightfully flustered when they'd bumped into each other at the Pink Bean for the first time? The blush that had suffused Jill's cheeks was etched into Amelia's memory. Or maybe it was the feel of Jill's hand, so warm and vital, in Amelia's own as she'd dressed her cut. The almost-kiss they'd nearly shared.

Amelia put her hand on her chest. Her heart was hammering away—totally normal after such a hot bath. The only conclusion she could draw with certainty was that Amelia hadn't fallen for Jill at first sight. It had happened slowly, almost imperceptibly. But fallen for Jill, she most certainly had.

Dating Jill probably wasn't the best course of action to aid her recovery, but wasn't she feeling better already? More alive? In fact… Amelia slid her hand up the curve of her breast. The previous time she had tried this, her body had responded with a resounding no. With an apathy so glaring it had frightened Amelia into thinking she might never experience the delight of arousal again. Until last night. Kissing Jill had popped goose bumps so fierce Amelia expected her skin might never recover. When she had surrendered to that kiss, and her brain hadn't acted up, had allowed her body to enjoy the exquisite sensation of Jill's soft lips against hers, all the arousal Amelia had not been able to feel for long, dreary months, seemed to catch up with her in a matter of minutes.

Could this be replicated? Was the memory of Jill's kiss, of Amelia's hand in her hair, of the intimacy of being pressed together like that in a passionate lip-lock, be enough to tip her over the edge she hadn't come close to since long before she'd been officially diagnosed?

There was only one way to find out.

Amelia closed her eyes and imagined it was Jill's hand cupping her breast. Jill's fingers skimming over her erect nipple. Jill's other hand stroking her belly, dipping lower.

On the back of her eyelids, she saw Jill's bright blue eyes looking back at her. Had Jill done this to herself while thinking of Amelia? The possibility made Amelia's hand dip lower, made her spread her legs a little wider. Had Jill called out her name as she brought herself to climax? The thought was exhilarating. To have that effect on a woman like Jill. Although, apparently, all Amelia had had to do was sit in a chair opposite her. She catalogued the thought as something to tease Jill with next time she saw her, and hopefully many more times to come.

Next, Amelia relived the sensation of her lips skating along the skin of Jill's neck. She'd come close to cupping Jill's breast, but something had stopped her.

In her head, right now, nothing was stopping her. In the safety of her own mind, she could strip Jill of her clothes. She could pretend that the nipple she was touching was Jill's instead of hers. She could pretend it was Jill emitting a low groan, finding it impossible to keep it locked inside her.

Soon, Amelia wasn't gauging her levels of arousal any longer. It was no longer a matter of whether she was aroused or not. It was now a matter of when, not if, she would reach orgasm. The previous impossibility of it had become hard to imagine now that her brain had latched on to all things Jill. As an added bonus, Amelia expected her body not to betray her by shutting down next time she and Jill kissed. No more alarm bells. Just surrendering to delicious moment after moment with Jill.

"Oh, Jill," Amelia crooned as a delicate but unmistakable wave of pleasure rolled through her. Just as when she had settled into the tub earlier, it seemed to originate in the remaining knots in her shoulders, loosening them even further, and roll throughout her flesh, releasing a bunch of feel-good hormones—under any other circumstance, Amelia could name them—that she had forgotten her very own body could produce.

She lay on the bed a while longer, panting and smiling, and thinking of Jill, who might not be her therapist any longer, but who had kick-started her healing process nonetheless.

Chapter Twenty-Seven

Just as it was impossible for Jill to switch off being a therapist when she was with Amelia—even in the throes of the most passionate kiss of her life—it was equally hard to accomplish when talking to Hera. The biggest difference at this point was that Jill knew much more about Hera than she did about Amelia. After all, she had been Hera's therapist for many years.

Hera, on a break from installing a new bathroom for Kristin and Sheryl, was sitting across from Jill at the Pink Bean.

"Admittedly, it is a bit weird to see you here instead of next door," Hera said. "Although now I get to ask you all the questions I want."

The front door opened, and Amber walked in. From what Jill had witnessed, Amber spent even more time at the Pink Bean than she did. Since they'd met at Liz and Jessica's, Amber and Jill had gone from distant smiles to a few conversations about nothing in particular. Amber walked over to their table as though she and Jill were much more than acquaintances.

"Just the woman I need to see," Amber said, looking at Hera, not Jill.

"I hear that a lot." Hera shot Amber a smile. "Believe it or not."

"Oh, I believe it." Amber glanced at their coffee cups, then at Jill. "Hi, Jill. How are you? I don't mean to be rude, but I have an emergency plumbing situation at the studio."

"If it's an emergency, surely you've called a plumber." Hera grinned.

"I tried. The earliest they can come is this afternoon. In the meantime, no one can use the toilet." Amber wrinkled her nose, and looked more closely at Jill and Hera. "Gosh, I'm so rude. I'm not interrupting anything, am I? I'm so sorry. I'm in a right state. I knew you would be here, Hera. Kristin told me after class this morning. I know you're not a plumber Hera, but would you have time to take a look?"

"Tell you what." Hera clearly took pride in being needed in this way. "I'll stop by in half an hour to see how I can be of help."

Amber put a hand on Hera's shoulder. "Thank you so much. You're a real lifesaver." She sent them both a smile. "Can I get you another coffee?"

They both shook their heads.

"Thanks again." With a smile, Amber turned and headed for the counter.

"Funny how you can tell someone has never lost a loved one because they call you a lifesaver for possibly fixing their clogged up toilet," Hera said.

"People say all sorts of things in everyday conversation," Jill offered.

Hera chuckled. "I guess they do."

"You're keeping busy."

"I am, because let me tell you something, Jill. The cliché

of lesbians being handy is utterly incorrect. Or maybe it's the crowd I hang with these days, with their fine art and designer clothes. In my younger days, I used to be friends with a bunch of women who'd all done up their own houses."

"Maybe it's an age thing. Once you're past forty, you have other priorities."

"And you want things done for you instead of doing them yourself." Hera nodded. "It's good for business."

"I guess we're both in a profession that won't easily disappear. Not even when the robots take over."

"I wouldn't be so sure of that." Hera stretched her arm over her head. "A robot's muscles don't ache like mine in the evening. A robot has endless energy and doesn't need a cup of strong coffee every hour."

"That may be so, but a robot will never have a human brain."

"Look, Doc, I'm perfectly willing to discuss the further automatization of our future lives, but right now, I'd honestly much prefer to catch up with you. How are things?"

"Things are…" *So good I'm nearly bursting out of my skin.* Although Kat had warned her not to share her feelings for Amelia with Hera, so much had changed since Jill's last conversation with Kat. In fact, Jill was pretty sure that next time she received an invitation to spend an evening with a bunch of coupled-up lesbians, she wouldn't be attending alone. Amelia had already agreed to go to the next Griffith-Porter art show with her, where she was sure to turn some heads. "I've met someone."

"Ha. I knew it," Hera said. "Kat thinks she's so discreet. As if I can't read her like an open book. And actually…" Hera regarded Jill intently. "There's something different about you, although that could be attributed to us meeting in this setting instead of your office. Anyway, tell me more."

"I'm not sure I should. It's still very early days."

"Whatever you're comfortable with."

"She's the most beautiful woman I've ever laid eyes on." Jill was aware of how utterly cheesy that sounded, but she didn't care.

"That's usually how it starts." Hera emitted a low chuckle.

"I should mention she's a former client."

"Really. Is that allowed?"

"Absolutely not, but that doesn't mean it never happens. I — Well, after making a right tit of myself during a session, it became impossible for me to continue to treat her."

Hera sat there grinning. "In a way, it's comforting to know that even someone like yourself can crack under a particular kind of pressure. That you're not this perfect specimen of humanity."

"In therapy, I behave a certain way for a reason. I'm not there to show my own emotions. I'm there for the client."

"Don't I know it. The number of times I attempted a joke and you hardly responded." Hera sipped from her coffee. "I thought my sense of humor was the problem." Hera didn't give the impression of doubting her own sense of humor at all.

"Clients often use humor as armor, to save themselves from having to dig deep. It's an easy enough shield to wield."

"And it's your job to see through all of that. I get it." Hera nodded. Jill guessed she agreed so easily because Hera had been in therapy for a long time—since before her partner had died. "Tell me more about your former client. Would I have run into her in the waiting room?"

Jill shook her head. "Her name's Amelia. She's crazy about soccer. She lives in Darlinghurst and is looking to start a soccer team consisting of women over forty only."

"For real?" Hera's eyes lit up.

"For very real." Jill studied Hera's face. "Are you interested?" Hera had never mentioned playing soccer.

"If it's anything like riding a bicycle, I should have some technique left. I used to play, but it's been a while. You know how it goes. I've been thinking about taking up a team sport to match my more outgoing personality these days." She sat there brimming. "As much as I like Amber, I'm not one for yoga and all that woo-woo stuff. Give me a field of grass beneath my feet and a ball to kick around."

"Sounds like I should introduce you to Amelia."

"I would like that very much," Hera said. "What position does she play?"

"Keeper."

"How about you, Doc? Are you thinking of joining your new girlfriend's team?"

Girlfriend? Was Amelia her girlfriend now? They'd only been on one official date. But it wasn't the number of dates they'd gone on that should define their status to each other. And Jill liked the sound of being Amelia's girlfriend very much. "Me?" She chuckled. "No way."

"Why not? You should try. What do you do for exercise?"

"Hm… walk to work."

"And to relax after a long day of listening to the woes of the likes of me?" Hera grinned.

"I have many ways of relaxing. I just can't imagine myself running after a ball. It seems so utterly pointless and I barely know the rules."

"Offside's a bit tricky, but it's not rocket science. You're a doctor. I'm sure you'd get the hang of it soon enough."

"I had no idea you were so keen to see me embarrass myself," Jill joked.

"I'm just a little excited. Please, do tell Amelia to get in touch."

"Put two of my former clients in touch so you can dish the dirt on me behind my back?" Jill said.

"You know it, Doc. You know it."

Somehow, Jill didn't mind that prospect at all. On the contrary, it might just prove that various kinds of relationships were possible with former clients.

Chapter Twenty-Eight

"You should kiss me again straight away," Jill said. "Because I might just have recruited someone for your 40+ soccer team."

"Really?" Amelia needed no incentive to kiss Jill again, so she did, although she was also very curious about her prospective future teammate.

"Her name's Hera and… she's a former client," Jill said.

"Hm." Amelia toyed with Jill's hand. "Do I detect some sort of pattern here?"

"I've no idea what you're referring to." Jill batted her lashes ostentatiously.

"What team does she belong to?" Amelia was much more interested in finding out about this Hera than in teasing Jill.

"None. She hasn't played in a while."

"But she has experience?"

"Yes. Is that an absolute requirement?" Jill asked.

"Beggars can't be choosers, I guess, but it's a plus. I can hardly afford to organize tryouts, can I? There isn't exactly a queue of women over forty eager to join a new soccer team."

"How about I bring her to your next home game?"

"You and a possible new teammate ogling me from the sidelines. I can hardly wait." Amelia kissed Jill again. Her interest in kissing Jill—and what came after that—was growing and growing. "It's lovely that you've been recruiting for me. It makes me feel so… cared for."

"I happen to care for you a great deal."

"Is that why you came tonight?" Amelia made sure her voice sounded extra sultry—she had noticed how Jill seemed to go all soft at that. "To care for me?"

Jill nodded. "In any way you want me to."

Before Amelia kissed Jill again, she paused… "I—um." She found Jill's gaze. "Previous experience has taught me that addressing this subject with you can be a bit… explosive, so I must be careful."

"What do you mean?" Jill grinned.

"Last Sunday, the day after our wonderful date I… tried touching myself again." It was a pure delight to study Jill's face while confiding this. It wasn't difficult and awkward like the first time Amelia had tried talking to Jill about masturbation—when she'd still been Jill's client and Jill had had to excuse herself because her lovestruck brain hadn't been able to process the information. "I can confirm that everything's very much in working order."

"You're right. Previously, I haven't dealt with you talking about this very well. On the contrary. But I'm a different person now. I've kissed you. I've wooed you. And I have a plan for you."

Amelia's delight only grew. "A plan? What do you mean?"

"You'll see, but—" The grin slipped off Jill's lips. "Seriously, Amelia. We will only do this if and when you're sure you're ready. I'm not here to push you into anything."

"Oh, I'm ready." Amelia was more than ready for the

real-life experience of all the things she had imagined Jill doing to her. And now she was talking about a plan? "Every last cell in my body is so very ready." She pulled Jill close. "How about you?"

"I am, too." Jill's voice was solemn. "I'm so in love with you, Amelia." Her voice wavered a touch. "I'm pretty much beside myself to be here with you right now."

"I guess the fact that you have a plan speaks of your eagerness." Amelia pressed her lips to the soft patch of skin just below Jill's ear. "If we're both ready," she whispered. "Let's go to the bedroom."

Amelia could claim to be ready all she wanted. She might have been able to bring herself to climax after a relaxing hot bath and while her blood was still suffused with feel-good hormones from her evening with Jill. But opening herself up to another woman, body and soul, might still very well be a hurdle she couldn't take on. She would only know for sure if she tried—and she *really* wanted to try. With Jill. She trusted Jill and there was no doubt about Jill's feelings for her. And Jill had *a plan*.

The first part of Jill's plan, apparently, consisted of them kissing profusely against the bedroom door—nothing Amelia wouldn't have planned herself.

"Can I get your explicit permission to take the lead on this?" Jill asked, after she'd caught her breath.

Amelia couldn't help but chuckle. "I'm sorry, but no one has ever asked me that before."

"I'm making a mental note as we speak to dig deeper into that later." Jill put her hands on Amelia's sides. "Much later." She hooked her fingers under Amelia's jeans.

"You have my permission for everything." The touch of

Jill's fingers on the sensitive skin there made Amelia's breath halt in her throat.

Jill responded by gently dragging the back of her fingers over Amelia's belly along the edge of her jeans. She stopped at the button, then flipped it open.

Whatever Jill's plan was, Amelia hoped it took into consideration that she hadn't been touched like this in a long time. And the last time she had been touched in a sexual way, it hadn't been by someone like Jill. Amelia had only had a few sessions of therapy, but they were enough for her to guess that her previous selection of bed partners had been yet another way in which she chose not to nourish herself. Already, with Jill, it felt so different. Like an act that would give something vital back to her instead of taking from her, that would restore her instead of leaving her emptier than before.

Jill's words echoed in the back of her mind. *I'm so in love with you.* Amelia hadn't said it out loud, but her reply was just as clear in her head: right back at you.

Jill unzipped Amelia's jeans. Her breasts pressed against Amelia's. Their lips found each other again and again. Amelia was starting to wonder what she'd been so worried about. Had she really pulled away from Jill mere days ago? The madness of it. But she had to trust that she'd done it for the right reasons—that she hadn't been ready. She was ready now.

Jill tugged at Amelia's jeans.

Suddenly, her jeans were an unbearable barrier, and Amelia gladly gave her a hand to remove them. Once she'd stepped out of her shoes and jeans, Amelia went to work on Jill's clothes. Soon, they were naked from the waist down, only protected by the sheer fabric of their panties. Amelia had dug up a pair of fancy ones she hadn't worn in months, but she'd guessed, correctly, that tonight, the occasion called for it.

She tried to pay attention to Jill's underwear—maroon silk, she thought—but she only had eyes for her face. Something in Jill's expression had changed. Her gaze was dominated by sheer hunger, her parted lips and narrowed eyes screamed out how much she wanted Amelia.

Amelia had previously felt wanted in her life, and she had never thought of herself as undesirable, but there was something magical about Jill, whom she had allowed a glimpse into the darkness of her soul, wanting her like this. The magic existed solely because it was the two of them together, the combination of their selves, their stories, and what had brought them together.

Jill pulled Amelia toward the bed.

Did the fact Jill had asked 'to take charge' mean Amelia had to restrain herself from doing exactly what she wanted to do? After they'd tumbled onto the bed, she'd wanted to get Jill's top off her as quickly as possible. Amelia wanted to see more of her. She wanted to run a finger along the cup of Jill's bra. She wanted to hold her breasts in her hands. But Amelia decided she would trust in Jill's judgment. Besides, it was a lovely feeling to be in bed with someone whose main aim appeared to be taking care of her.

Jill's fingers skimmed over Amelia's blouse and danced around the buttons.

Faster. Amelia decided to speed things along by pulling it over her head instead of having Jill slowly unbutton it. Too bad if that wasn't part of Jill's plan.

"Jesus." Jill had stilled somewhat. The expression on her face was still one of pure and utter want, however. "You're so beautiful," she murmured. She placed her hand on Amelia's side and caressed her naked skin with two fingers, before skating them up toward the swell of Amelia's breast. Her fingertips dipped under the fabric of Amelia's bra.

Amelia's nipple reacted instantly, almost painfully, straining hard against the cup. She stopped herself from taking off her bra there and then. Instead, she focused on Jill again. On the lust in her glance—how could a woman who looked so overtaken by her own desire even stick to a plan? She focused on how much she wanted Amelia. How she clearly adored her. And on how Jill's obvious adoration of her infused Amelia with a touch more regard for herself.

A gasp escaped Amelia's throat as Jill's fingertips retreated from Amelia's bra and she made quick work of hoisting her own top over her head and tossing it somewhere into the room.

Jill's bra matched her panties and Amelia took a few seconds to admire how the maroon lingerie contrasted so deliciously with Jill's creamy skin. It was flattering that Jill had dressed up for her—with the very prospect of this in mind.

A haze blurred Amelia's vision as Jill came for her again. It was all touch now as Jill folded her arms tightly around Amelia, as though she wanted to pull her as close as humanly possible. One minute they were kissing with Jill's hands roaming wildly through Amelia's hair; the next Jill was breathing into her ear, whispering how crazy Amelia was driving her.

Then, Jill pulled away. She took a deep breath, possibly to calm herself. She briefly closed her eyes, then studied Amelia's bed. She sat back against the headboard, then held out her arms. "Come here, please," she said, her voice thick with desire.

Amelia moved toward Jill, ready to press herself against Jill's naked body again.

"Wait," Jill whispered. "Turn around and lie in my arms with your back to me."

This must be part of the plan. Amelia arched up her eyebrows. She didn't want to look away from Jill. She wanted to see as much of her as possible.

"Please." Jill's glance emitted a plea so lusty and heartfelt, Amelia couldn't help but obey. Jill was here for her but she was also there for Jill. They were in this bed together and for each other.

Heart pounding, Amelia swiveled her body around until she was sitting between Jill's legs, with her back to her.

"Lean back," Jill whispered.

Amelia lowered herself into Jill's arms. The fabric of Jill's bra was soft and enticing against the skin of her back.

"Close your eyes," Jill said. "Just relax and enjoy."

Amelia let her head rest on Jill's shoulder feeling the puff of Jill's breath on her cheek. Amelia allowed herself to relax, to stifle the self-consciousness that she felt at lying in this unfamiliar position in Jill's arms. To just let go and trust in Jill.

Jill ran her fingertips over Amelia's upper arms, leaving an expanse of goose bumps in their wake. Jill's fingers gravitated toward Amelia's breasts, but they stayed chastely above her bra this time around. Perhaps Jill had gotten a bit carried away earlier. Perhaps she had strayed from her plan. The thought brought a smile to Amelia's lips. Maybe Amelia facing away from Jill was part of the plan, because the face always gave so much away. The downside was that Amelia couldn't kiss Jill.

But wait… Jill's fingertips travelled across Amelia's neck, up to her jaw. She pressed against it and Amelia turned her head sideways, where her lips found Jill's.

Amelia's lips latched onto Jill's, as though she never wanted them to break apart again. As though breathing in fresh air had become obsolete now that they had found each other, now that they were in bed together, and Jill's other hand was roaming across Amelia's cleavage, her fingertips straying in the direction of Amelia's breasts, but not quite going there. The teasing of Jill's fingers, mixed with the intensity of their kiss—which grew in fierceness again by the second—didn't miss its mark on Amelia's body. Every cell in her body was wide awake and alert to Jill's touch.

Then Jill's hand ventured lower. Her fingertips danced along the sensitive skin of Amelia's inner thigh, before inching closer to her panties. But as with her breasts, Jill steered clear of Amelia's hottest spots. She just let her fingers explore and tease and drive Amelia wilder as the seconds and minutes ticked along.

Amelia dug her own fingertips into Jill's legs. Right now, it was only increasing desire coursing through her veins, but if Jill kept this up, it would soon turn into frustration. Although Amelia understood what Jill was trying to do. She was making sure Amelia's body was as ready as her words had claimed. Jill must know like no other that sometimes words weren't always accurate, that words sometimes lacked in what they could convey. That the real truth could be spoken only by the body—and Amelia's body had suffered a burnout just as much as her brain had.

Arousal was as much in the mind as the body—Jill must know that. And Amelia's desire might already be awakened, but Jill wanted to make sure Amelia's body was on the same level as her desire. That it could react in a way that would bring her the most pleasure.

Jill perhaps wanted to reduce the risk of Amelia putting a stop to this because, in the end, she might not be as ready as she had believed herself to be. Jill was smart—just as smart as Amelia was when her brain was fully functioning. Maybe after tonight, after Jill had had her way with her, it might reach its peak again soon.

But that wasn't why Amelia had invited Jill into her bedroom. She was here because Amelia wanted her and, ultimately, all the other stuff, when it came down to it, didn't matter. All that mattered was that they were together, exposing their truest selves to each other.

The soft, unrelenting touch of Jill's fingers made Amelia squirm. Her desire grew and grew. Underneath her panties, which Jill still seemed reluctant to touch, wetness gathered between Amelia's legs. Her clit throbbed wildly.

She turned her face toward Jill again. Jill gazed down at her for an instant, then leaned in and kissed her. As their lips touched, Jill's fingertips skated along Amelia's panties. It was a featherlight touch, but Amelia felt it in every fiber of her being, it reverberated through the tiniest of her muscles, because Jill had been driving her crazy with her delicate caresses, full of intention but with no follow-through.

Amelia groaned into Jill's mouth. Surely Jill must know how ready Amelia was—she was about to spontaneously combust.

But Jill kissed her again, her tongue as soft in Amelia's mouth as her touch along her panties. While the sweep of Jill's tongue inside Amelia's mouth remained more tentative than claiming, her fingertips pressed a bit harder between Amelia's legs. And then, finally, she drew a circle around Amelia's aching clit.

Stars wheeled and danced in front of her eyes and she found it hard to focus. Her breath stopped in her throat. Her heart might as well have given out completely. She wanted Jill's touch on her more than she wanted life itself. Admittedly, that was a slight exaggeration, but what was life without this? Without the flames of desire fanning high and wide inside of her, warming her muscles, breathing life back into her from her very core? Life had been colorless and utterly bland, until now, until it wasn't anymore.

When Amelia closed her eyes, life blazed on the back of her eyelids in full technicolor. And Jill was only touching her clit above her panties.

"Please, Jill," she breathed into her mouth. "I want to take them off."

"Wait," Jill whispered.

Before Amelia had a chance to complain, Jill moved her hand to the waistband of Amelia's panties, and slipped it inside. The pulse that throbbed in her body picked up speed. Her heart hammered against her ribcage. She feared she might forget how to breathe altogether as Jill's fingers inched closer to her clit. However, they bypassed it to dip even lower, between Amelia's eager lips.

"You're so wet," Jill whispered, her voice a hoarse, desire-drenched croak. "Fuck."

Amelia didn't have the wherewithal to say, 'yes please', but she didn't need to. Jill pressed herself against Amelia's neck as her fingers slid inside Amelia's wetness. Because of the position they were in, Jill's fingers couldn't thrust very deeply, but it was more than enough to lift Amelia onto an even higher plane of arousal.

There was no friction as Jill's fingers slid upward through Amelia's wetness, and Jill slowly circled Amelia's clit.

Amelia's muscles tensed. She wouldn't need too many of those circles before she exploded into a massive climax. As if she could sense her heightened arousal—it was probably pretty obvious—Jill withdrew her fingertip all the way out of Amelia's panties.

"I want to see you," Jill said, as she gently pushed Amelia off her and maneuvered herself from behind Amelia "When I fuck you."

Amelia didn't wait for Jill to remove her panties. She

threw them behind her somewhere, probably onto a pillow, and drew Jill on top of her. She wrapped Jill in her arms, drowning in the sensation of warmth and heat that having another person on top of her ignited. Amelia's entire body pulsed with desire, screamed for some sort of release, yet in that moment, all she wanted to do was kiss Jill, let their tongues meet over and over again.

But Amelia was not in charge—she'd given all the power to Jill earlier when she had asked for it. And Jill's hand drifted downward again, only briefly halting at Amelia's still bra-clad breasts. Maybe she was saving the baring of Amelia's chest for later. Maybe she wanted a touch of mystery to remain between them.

With a small, secret smile, Jill slipped off her, her warm body still glued to Amelia's side. Her fingertips danced across Amelia's inner thigh again, but they only teased her briefly this time around.

There was no way she would resist. Amelia spread her legs for Jill. The air between her legs roused another round of goose bumps on her skin.

Jill's finger slipped through her wetness. She gave a few tentative strokes, sliding, gauging, lightly brushing Amelia's clit, before her fingers slipped inside.

Amelia threw her head back into the pillows and her eyes fell shut, but she could still feel Jill's gaze on her. It burned through her closed eyelids. It worked in tandem with the thrust of Jill's fingers inside. Amelia placed her hand against Jill's back and held on tight. This was nothing like the other day, after her bath, when she'd imagined Jill doing this exact thing to her. The difference was night and day. Not only because Amelia didn't have to rely on her own imagination to create the sensation, but even more so because of the connection it forged between them. To let another woman in like this hadn't been possible for Amelia while she'd been going through her dark spell. Did the fact that she was enjoying this so excruciatingly much mean that she was cured? That she could start looking forward again instead of disappearing into a sea of gloominess that always held her back?

Jill brought Amelia back into her body in a way that she hadn't been able to achieve on her own. Amelia had always known that the body needed as much attention as the brain, which was one of the reasons she'd always latched onto soccer with such enthusiasm, and she trained just as hard as the forwards and the defenders, even though, as the goal-keeper, she could easily have afforded to slack off. But Jill pushing her fingers high inside her, was of another order of bodily ecstasy altogether. This, Amelia suspected, might be the very thing she needed to truly come back to herself. A woman like Jill taking care of her the way she had done since the first moment they'd met. A woman like Jill loving and adoring her. A woman like Jill to love and adore in return.

Jill amped up the energy of her strokes and brought her thumb into play, edging it along Amelia's clit every time she drove deep inside her. Amelia opened her eyes, and found Jill's eyes looking back at her, the gleaming blue of them, endless pools of compassion and lust. Jill's mouth was slightly agape with effort. Her entire face was a mask of concentration, her entire being focused on one task only: making Amelia feel good.

A groan of pleasure came from her mouth. If there was any doubt left in her mind that she could do this, that she could tip over that imaginary edge of pure delight, it quickly disappeared as the first wave washed over her. Although entirely expected, its sheer force still took her by surprise. The power with which her muscles tensed and unclenched left her breathless, exhausted and utterly spent.

Amelia clamped hard around Jill's dexterous fingers. She

held them deep inside of her as pleasure engulfed her, relaxed and restored her. Tears gathered behind her eyes. Amelia might have taken sharing her bed with another woman for granted for the largest part of her adult life, but she no longer did so now. This thing with Jill was special. Amelia hadn't been ready to let someone into her life and her bedroom, yet here she was. Here she lay, recovering after her first climax in a very long time brought about by another person. Amelia's intuition gathered strength on the back of her climax and she knew, with a deep certainty, that Jill wouldn't be going anywhere any time soon.

Chapter Twenty-Nine

Jill was in the stage between sleeping and waking, that in-between time just before she came to her full senses. Part of her wanted to remain asleep for fear that all of last night had been a dream and that she'd wake up in her own bed, Amelia nowhere to be seen.

The other part of her wanted to open her eyes and see Amelia lying next to her, her long hair fanned out around her face, her sultry lips swollen from the endless kissing—and so much more—they'd engaged in the night before. What would Amelia's voice sound like first thing in the morning? Jill couldn't wait to find out. What a dream last night had been. To witness Amelia yield under her touch, to hold her afterward when emotion got the better of her. And after that, when Amelia had bestowed all her affections on Jill, and then some. It was as though she could still feel Amelia's lips everywhere. Jill was barely awake and already her body was yearning for Amelia again. Already she was raring to go—not bad for someone about to turn fifty.

Jill dragged herself from the last remnants of sleep, all her senses slowly adjusting and gearing up for another day.

But wait. What was that? Was she dreaming she was waking up while she was actually still asleep? It wouldn't be the first time that had happened to her. She must still be asleep because she could very much feel Amelia's lips skimming her thigh, climbing upward, to the spot that hadn't stopped thrumming, or so it seemed, since Jill had been invited into Amelia's bedroom. Jill had zero incentive to wake up from this particular dream.

Miraculously, it felt as good as the real thing, which she had experienced more than once last night. Amelia's soft lips on her, taking her to ultimate bliss. But, hold on… was that the alarm clock on her phone that went off every weekday morning at seven? Why was her phone spoiling her dream?

"Do you want to get that?" Amelia's muffled voice came from under the covers.

Wide awake now, Jill lifted the covers and looked into Amelia's face peeking up from between her legs. Goodness. It was real. And it was much better than any dream Jill had ever had.

She found her phone and turned off the alarm.

"Sorry." She smiled down at Amelia, who didn't appear in a hurry to leave her spot between Jill's legs. "And good morning."

"Morning." Amelia half-smiled. "I have a much better way to wake you up than the alarm on your phone."

"I agree it's infinitely better."

"Do you need to leave?" Amelia asked. "I wouldn't want you to keep a client waiting."

"My first appointment is at nine thirty." Jill had double-checked before going to sleep last night. "We have time."

"Good." Amelia all but licked her lips. "Because I have *a plan* for you this morning." She threw the covers off her. "But now that you're awake, let me wish you a proper good morning first."

To have Amelia crawl up to her like that, fully naked, her body still warm with sleep, was the next in what seemed to Jill an endless array of delights when she was in Amelia's company.

Amelia nested in the crook of her shoulder. "Did you sleep well?"

"Oh, yes. And I had quite the dream as well." As lovely as it was to snuggle up to Amelia, the circumstances in which Jill had woken had left her very frisky. "You had a starring role in it." She turned toward Amelia and kissed her on the lips. "Did you get some sleep?"

"I slept so well and so deeply, I think I will need you to sleep here with me every night."

"That might not be down to me being here but more to what we did before we went to sleep." Jill couldn't help bursting into a smile.

"Then we'll have to do that again tonight as well," Amelia said.

Last night certainly hadn't been a dream. Amelia was already talking about doing it again. Jill had no arguments against that. She couldn't wait to get back here tonight and do it all over.

"In fact… I think I'll finish what I started now," Amelia said. "Make sure you're properly awake before you go to work." Amelia kissed her cheek, then kissed her way down Jill's neck. She halted at Jill's peaked nipples, leaving them much harder than before.

She continued her path of featherlight kisses, dotting them liberally around Jill's skin. Despite the early hour, Jill's body quickly went into overdrive, as though it had stored up an endless supply of arousal and Amelia held the only key to unlock it. Amelia, whom she wasn't supposed to be with, but who was now showering her in the most divine kisses. Jill had never stood a chance against Amelia, although she could hardly blame it on Amelia's charms—charming another woman had been the last item on Amelia's list the first time she'd met Jill.

Amelia's long, soft hair trailed in the wake of her kisses, caressing Jill's skin all over again.

Jill spread her legs a little wider.

Amelia's lips trailed along her thighs now.

The pulsating throb between Jill's legs tripled in intensity. Just as her mind hadn't stood a chance against Amelia's appearance that first time she'd stepped into her office, Jill's resolve was worthless against the onslaught of Amelia's lips on her now. She kissed Jill close to and then around her clit. Jill couldn't wait to feel Amelia's tongue on her. Her entire being was poised toward that imminent, delicious touch. Jill already knew what it felt like when Amelia licked her there. She knew it would make her blood sparkle and her flesh sing. But Amelia waited until Jill started squirming underneath her, her desire so ramped up, she didn't know what to do with it anymore. Then, at last, Amelia's tongue skated along her lips and circled around her clit. A fresh jolt of fire ran underneath Jill's skin. Heat bubbled up from her core and caused an avalanche, a proper heat storm, in her flesh, inundating every last one of her cells. When Amelia licked her, her tongue gentle, almost tentative at first, lapping at her, Jill's entire body responded.

Even when, at the start, she had known full well it was in everyone's best interest that she got over her silly crush on her hot client as quickly as possible, Jill had dreamed of moments like this over and over again. Of Amelia's luscious mane of hair draped over Jill's belly while Amelia did the very thing she was doing right now and, of course, it had stoked her feelings for Amelia instead of lessening them.

And now, Jill didn't want to get over her. She wanted anything but that. And because that's just how life was sometimes, when the universe fully conspired in your favor. Jill was in the middle of experiencing her dream in exquisite real-life detail. The silken softness of Amelia's tongue, now coming at her with intensified pressure. The divine sounds Amelia produced while she was pleasuring Jill, as though the greater pleasure was all hers—it couldn't possibly be. Amelia's hands holding her tightly, as though needing to keep her in place—as though it was even conceivable that Jill ever wanted to get out of this particular situation.

Within a few fast minutes, Amelia had brought Jill to the brink once again. Her tongue action was delicious and exquisitely adept, but much more than Amelia's prowess, it was the simple fact that it was her down there, doing this to Jill, that had by far the greatest effect. The woman Jill had silently and then not-so-silently adored from the first minute she'd met her, the woman she'd desired like perhaps no other before. It was more than plenty for Jill to bury her hands in Amelia's dark hair, to let its improbable softness engulf her with all things Amelia, and surrender to Amelia's tongue as it brought her to effortless climax.

Jill cried out loudly and unabashedly—this was not the kind of pleasure to be reined in. This was the kind of delight that needed to be screamed out, shouted from the rooftops, made known to all of Sydney, all of Australia, why not the entire world? Because Jill was madly in love and of course she knew that a couple of orgasms shared between them didn't magically make it mutual, yet Jill knew that it was. She sensed it. She felt it crackle in the air between them. She picked up on it when she looked in Amelia's eyes. And wasn't that the greatest delight of all?

Chapter Thirty

THERE WAS a definite lightness to Amelia's tread. She wondered if it could make her jump higher, reach that little bit farther, when a ball was aimed at her goal. In the state she was in, lovestruck and deeply satisfied sexually, she figured it just might.

She was the first to arrive at the pitch where the Darlinghurst Darlings played their home games. Granted, she was early. Warm-up wouldn't start for half an hour. But it had been impossible to stay home for longer.

Jill had an appointment before she could come see the match. Amelia had too much unexpected-but-welcome energy racing through her to lazily linger alone in Jill's bed. If she were less smitten, she might have harnessed it to unleash during the game, but who was she kidding? She was the goalkeeper. She didn't have to run up and down the pitch over and over again for ninety minutes. She had to keep hawk-like eyes on the goings-on in front of her and guard her goal. Try to stop a penalty if it was that kind of game. Before Sophia had joined, Kate, their coach, who was really just another team member of the Darlings and played as center back, usually asked Amelia to execute any free kicks—being the goalie she was able to cover long distances as well as having the right technique. However, nowadays Sophia's technique was better than Amelia's and there was no use sulking over that—Amelia wasn't the kind of person to put her own ego before a win for the team.

Despite the balmy spring temperature, she broke into a light jog around the pitch to keep her muscles warm. Considering Sophia's contribution to the team also made Amelia think about Sophia's overt flirting. Amelia had never really participated in Sophia's banter, nor had she reciprocated the flirting. At times, she'd been downright rude, because she had the overwhelming excuse of her burnout. Now that she was seeing Jill, however, that excuse was no longer valid. And Jill was coming to the game today. She imagined how that might make Sophia feel.

Given the chance, Amelia should probably try to have a conversation with Sophia before Jill arrived. But pre-game really wasn't the time for that. She'd hoped to seize the opportunity last Thursday at practice, but Sophia had been absent—again. Amelia picked up the pace of her jog. She hoped Sophia's no-show didn't mean she was contemplating leaving the Darlings—they needed her. On top of that, Amelia hoped fervently that if Sophia did decide to leave, it wouldn't be because of her.

She heard a car pull up in the parking lot. She jogged to the entrance of the grounds and did some leg stretches as she waited to see who of her teammates was as eager and early as her.

A woman in a white T-shirt with short gray hair and impressive muscle tone in her arms stood looking at the pitch. Maybe she was someone from the other team, although if she was, she must be new to the league, which was so small that Amelia knew most of the other players.

Amelia sized up the competition while she walked up to the stranger. At first glance, she looked to be in the right age bracket for her 40+ team. Amelia wondered what position she played, although, at this point, any player would do.

"The visitor locker room is through there," Amelia said, only then noticing that the woman wasn't carrying a kit bag. She didn't even have a purse on her.

"I'm here as a spectator." She cracked a smile. "But I'm a bit early. I've driven down from Bondi and I wanted to make sure to beat any traffic."

The amateur women's league games usually didn't attract many spectators apart from dragged-along family members and friends. Most people had better things to do on a Saturday morning.

"Supporting which team?"

"Hi, I'm Hera." The woman extended her hand. "My friend Jill is supposed to meet me here. I'm interested in joining the Darlinghurst Darlings."

"Oh." Amelia shook Hera's hand with vigor. Had Jill not said that Hera was also a former client of hers? "In that case, a warm welcome to our home ground. I'm Amelia. I'm... Jill's—" *Girlfriend?*

Before she had a chance to introduce herself as Jill's girlfriend for the first time, Hera said, "Oh yes, Jill's told me all about you. In fact, you're kind of the reason I'm here." Hera ran her gaze over Amelia unceremoniously. "I hear Jill's quite taken with you." A grin appeared on her lips.

"Is she now?" This was also the first time Amelia had met one of Jill's friends.

"Oh yes." Hera's eyes sparkled. "Did she tell you I was coming today?"

"She told me all about it." Amelia gave Hera a good once-over in response to the one she'd just been subjected to. Soccer-wise, she liked what she saw. "I've been looking forward to meeting you. New members are always very welcome."

"I haven't played soccer in a long time, but because of my job, my physical fitness is not too bad."

"Which position did you used to play?"

"Midfield, although back in the day, we all pretty much played every position. Women's soccer has taken great strides in the past decade."

"The fact that there are far more female pros these days has certainly increased the interest in the amateur leagues, but some Saturdays it's still difficult to put together a full team, even in a city like Sydney."

"I can imagine," Hera said. "I've been out of the game for more than ten years myself."

"Welcome back." Amelia didn't want to inquire as to why Hera had given up for so long. Even though Amelia couldn't imagine giving up the sport—she had clung to it even during the harshest days of her burnout—she knew it was different for most other people. People who had more going on in their lives than work and soccer alone. "Jill was worried that as two former clients of hers all we would do is gossip about her," she said instead.

"Honestly, when I was still Jill's client, I didn't know anything about her, apart from the fact that she loved expensive-looking artwork in her office. She doesn't give anything away. Even her body language is really hard to decipher, although I did know from the very beginning that she was a warm and kindhearted person. That's the sort of thing she can't hide."

Amelia couldn't explain why *her* chest was swelling with pride. She had nothing to do with how Jill conducted herself in therapy. But to hear someone else call Jill warm and kind made her feel good.

"I only had two and a half sessions with her, so..." Amelia snickered.

"God, I would have loved to be a fly on the wall for those." Hera had an easygoing smile. "Just to see Jill squirm a little. I can't really picture it. She's always been the very image of someone holding it together at all cost."

"Between us, she doesn't always." Amelia was probably speaking out of turn a bit, but it was fun to talk about Jill like this, with someone who knew her. She would introduce Jill to Dawn and the rest of the team later today.

Hera gave a hearty chuckle. "That's good to know."

The sound of more cars pulling up put a stop to their banter about Jill. Sophia was the next person to enter the grounds—and she wasn't alone.

"Let me introduce you to a few more Darlinghurst Darlings," Amelia said, while her gaze was drawn to Hera's impressive biceps again. She did say her job kept her fit. Had Jill mentioned what she did for a living? When Amelia's gaze flitted from Hera's arms to Sophia, she couldn't help but notice that Sophia was walking hand in hand with the woman she'd brought.

After she'd introduced Hera to Sophia and vice versa, Sophia, while ostentatiously holding up their joined hands, introduced the woman as 'her new squeeze' Yasmine. Things must be moving quickly then, Amelia thought, although she was also happy for Sophia. And for herself because she wouldn't need to have an awkward conversation. Sometimes, things miraculously solved themselves. How utterly amazing when that happened.

More women started to arrive and while they warmed up, Amelia kept an eye on the entrance, waiting for Jill to arrive.

She only showed up a few minutes before the referee

blew the whistle to start the game, leaving no time for the Darlinghurst Darlings' keeper to claim a good luck kiss.

The Darlings won the game three-nil—Sophia scoring twice, quite possibly doing her best to impress her 'new squeeze'—which allowed Amelia to keep a clean sheet in front of Jill. Perhaps she had also managed to impress *her* new squeeze. The difference between Yasmine and Jill being that Jill didn't run up to Amelia after the game and jump into her arms as though she were the second coming.

She and Dawn were set to meet Hera and Jill at the pub after they'd showered. Dawn seemed to be stalling. It took her forever to blow-dry her hair, which was something she usually didn't even bother with after a game.

"Although I can't wait to meet Jill, can we have a quick word before we join the others?" Dawn asked after Amelia had exited the locker room.

"Of course."

They stayed behind until they were alone, Amelia patiently waiting, although she was eager to throw her arms around Jill and celebrate the Darlings' victory with her.

"Did I miss the message that made today bring-your-new-lover-to-soccer day?" Dawn's voice was all cynical bitterness. "I knew Jill was coming, but I had no idea Sophia would be bringing that girl. Did you hear? She's still a student. Studying philosophy, apparently. Whoop-de-doo."

Amelia threw her arm around her friend. "Maybe you should have brought Cindy."

"She was supposed to come with the kids but Julian threw up all night. So much for your update on my life of glamour and glitz."

"Aw, Dawny, what's going on?"

"Just one of those days, you know."

"At least we won," Amelia said.

"That we did." There was some vigor in Dawn's nod. A win always managed to boost their morale.

"And we might have a new team member," Amelia added.

"If you don't whisk her away for your new team." Dawn sounded deflated again.

"Hm." Amelia sensed it wasn't the time to push Dawn on leaving the Darlings and starting the new team with her. "So what are we going to do about this jea—"

"Melly," Dawn interrupted her. "You know I love you and I want to support you in whatever it takes to get you going again, but I'm not sure I can ever leave the Darlings. They're my—*our*—team. We started it. We came up with its ridiculous name and everything."

"Okay." Maybe this wasn't about Sophia after all.

"Just… don't rush into anything. You've been through a lot and probably had all sorts of ideas running through your head. Trust me, I know how appealing a crazy, out-there idea can be when you're going through a rough time." She let her back fall against the wall. "I know this whole Sophia thing is utterly ridiculous and I know it's ludicrous that I'm jealous of her twenty-two-year-old girlfriend. But still, it offers me some sort of comfort. She's a thought I can turn to when the kids have been screaming their heads off all day long or when Cindy is short with me because she's tired. Maybe it's similar with you and the new team. It's a shiny new thing that offers distraction when you should actually be focusing on what you already have."

A knock came on the door. "Are you decent, ladies?" Steve, the caretaker of the ground, shouted from behind the closed door.

"Yes," Amelia and Dawn answered in unison.

"In that case, I'd like to lock up. I have somewhere to be. If you don't mind."

Amelia and Dawn gathered their belongings, said goodbye to Steve, and headed to the pub, which was only a few minutes away. Amelia used the few minutes of walking, and unexpected silence, to process what Dawn had just said. Maybe her friend was right. Maybe she should appreciate what she had—the team they had built and kept going through good times and bad—instead of wanting something new that, realistically, didn't even have that much chance of success.

When they arrived at the pub, Amelia clasped eyes on Jill sitting with Hera, both of them nursing a glass of wine. Warmth blossomed in Amelia's chest because now, she had someone to mull things like this over with.

"Lovely to meet you, Jill," Dawn said. "I've been Amelia's best friend forever and I'm here to answer all your questions."

Chapter Thirty-One

JILL SAID goodbye to her Thursday six-o'clock regular. She opened the door to let him out and did a double take when she spotted Amelia in the waiting area. They were supposed to meet at the Pink Bean in half an hour. From there they'd walk to the Griffith-Porter gallery together.

"I'm here for an emergency session," Amelia said, after Jill's client was out of earshot. "I hope you can spare the time." Her eyes sparkled with mischief.

"I'm supposed to meet someone in half an hour." Jill was more than happy to play along.

Amelia rose and all but pushed Jill into her office. After she closed the door behind them, she studied it. "Does this have a lock?"

"What kind of emergency session did you have in mind?" Jill double-locked the door, not that anyone would be barging in unexpectedly.

"You'll find out soon enough." Amelia smiled her lopsided, dizzying smile. She had dressed up in a spaghetti-strap top accentuating her exquisite shoulder line.

'Soon' couldn't come fast enough for Jill. "Is there a specific issue you would like to address?"

Amelia nodded and held out her hand. "Oh, yes. *Very* specific."

Jill took Amelia's hand and let herself be tugged closer. Amelia wrapped her arms around Jill's neck and kissed her with such fierce warmth, Jill forgot all about the opening they were supposed to attend. Whereas a few weeks earlier, a new exhibition at her favorite gallery would have been high-lighted in her calendar and something she'd be looking forward to, her priorities seemed to have shifted—or perhaps even reduced to a single one: Amelia.

As they kept kissing, Amelia walked them to the nearest wall and gently pushed Jill against it.

"I seem to have developed a new obsession, Doctor," Amelia whispered in her ear while she wasted no time undoing the buttons on Jill's blouse. "There's this woman I can't stop thinking about. I'm talking day and night here. Every second of every minute. My soccer career is suffering greatly." Amelia kissed her neck while she bared Jill's stomach.

"Who is this woman?" Jill said in between groans. "She must be quite something to have you"—Amelia's hands had traveled to her back and were fiddling with the clasp of her bra—"so enthralled."

"I'm pretty sure"—Amelia unhooked Jill's bra and stared at her chest while she first slid Jill's blouse off her arms, and then her bra—"she has me under some sort of spell. She's a psychiatrist and while I've never heard of anything like that occurring in any of the research journals I subscribe to, I can't know everything. Maybe you've heard of such a thing before?" Amelia heaved a small sigh—as though the sight of Jill's naked chest was exactly what she'd been waiting to see all day long—and gently cupped Jill's breasts in her hands, her fingers skimming along her nipples.

"Oh," Jill groaned. She was done playing along. This was what Amelia did to her. In a matter of minutes, she had her reduced to a puddle of pure lust. Amelia's lips were on her again, preventing Jill from speaking, anyway, for which she was more than glad. She buried her hands in Amelia's hair, not caring that they had somewhere to be. Just as Jill didn't care that her blouse was lying crumpled on the floor. All the things that had once mattered to her before were no longer important when she was with Amelia, when all she cared about was quenching the relentless hunger between her legs.

Amelia caressed her nipples, and Jill could feel herself flood once again. The heat in her core transformed into liquid warmth between her legs. Amelia kissed her way down to Jill's breasts, trailed a moist and delicious path to the side of her chest before her lips clasped wetly and heavenly around Jill's nipple.

Jill steadied herself against the wall. She had never done anything like this in her office. How would she focus on what her clients were saying with the memory of doing this lingering about? With the memory of Amelia, her former client, sucking her nipple deep into her mouth? Jill could feel the sweep of Amelia's tongue all the way into her core.

Amelia's hands meandered over her belly, making Jill's pulse pick up speed, its frantic rhythm reflected between her legs. Amelia flipped open the button to Jill's slacks and wasted no time unzipping her. Her lips remained on Jill's nipple, her tongue twirling. Her hand dipped down resolutely. A finger skated along Jill's panties. This was turning into a matter of acute urgency for Jill—maybe that was what Amelia had referred to earlier. This had been her intention all along. If it was symbolic for Jill that Amelia's finger was about to dive into her panties in her office, it must hold some meaning for Amelia as well. She had first entered here a partly broken woman, someone who needed fixing, or at the very least some guidance on how to make her life better. Jill hadn't been much help, yet here they stood.

Jill concluded that both their lives were infinitely better now. Sometimes meeting someone new was all it took—that and taking a chance at a time when you might not think it opportune. Jill had seen it over and over again. It was the very definition of life with all its ups and downs, its peaks and valleys with all the people that you met and lost and kept and rekindled a connection with along the way.

Amelia was someone to hang on to, although Jill had no crystal ball. But someone who could set her blood on fire just by aiming a smile at her, by saying a few choice words in that maddeningly low voice of hers, was not someone Jill would be prepared to lose anytime soon.

Then again, there had been a time when she would have said the same about Rasmus, who was now thousands of miles away. He was completely out of her life, because the course of a life, by definition, was unknowable. She silently wished him well.

From the second she had first clasped eyes on Amelia, Jill had known that something of Amelia would remain in her soul for the rest of her days on this planet. Silly as it might have been at the time, it had been that impactful. That, too, Jill had learned from years of experience: the silliest of things can often leave the biggest impact. The smallest occurrences can have the biggest consequences.

Like the minute action of Amelia's finger, drawing the lightest of circles around her clit, revving up Jill's arousal to the point where she could barely contain herself.

Amelia's lips had traveled from her nipple back to her ear. "I want you so much," she murmured, her voice dipping into its sexiest register.

Jill suspected that Amelia knew full well that it was an extra instrument to turn her on. Just like the finger in her panties, and her lips around Jill's nipple earlier, the sound of Amelia's distinct voice in her ear set off rounds of fireworks in her flesh.

Then, at last, Amelia's finger slipped inside her panties and slid through her wetness. Jill's knees buckled because what else could they do? Her body was under an attack of arousal. Amelia had whirled into her office like a tornado of lust, her eyes glinting with purpose, her only goal Jill's swift seduction.

Amelia's finger entered her and Jill's breath stalled. It always did when Amelia slipped into her, when she breached the very last border of intimacy.

Amelia's palm skated along Jill's pulsing clit. Every stroke of her fingers made Jill pant harder.

How was it even possible to want someone this much? To spend the better portion of the day dreaming of their fingers delving inside of you, when your brain should really be focusing on other things. But Amelia's strong, capable fingers were the stuff Jill's dreams were made of these days. And right now, those fingers were doing another magnificent job of taking her completely out of her head and transporting her to Amelia-land. To the place where only Amelia existed with her zealous love of soccer and her fierce, protective love for her friends Dawn and Cindy and her love for analytics and biometrics and scientific literature and now, perhaps, also her love for Jill.

Because in that moment Jill felt very loved by Amelia, although her sense of reality was heavily distorted by the climax burrowing its way through her muscles, rumbling through her flesh—like that very first lightning bolt that had struck her right in the heart.

She clung to Amelia's body while she came, while her entire being seemed to clasp itself around Amelia's fingers.

"Oh, fuck," Jill said, after she was able to speak again. She pulled Amelia so close she could feel her lips stretch into a smile against her cheek. "This is no way to behave in your therapist's office."

"Then let's get out of here so you can buy me some poncy art."

Chapter Thirty-Two

AMELIA'S HEART thudded in her throat. When she had last stepped into a therapist's office for the first time, it had ended up changing her life—and not in the way she had expected.

The door of Dr. Scarpa's office opened and a pleasant-looking woman appeared. For the life of her, Amelia couldn't remember what she'd thought of Jill's appearance when she'd first greeted her. She'd been just as nervous, if not more, so appraising her therapist's looks had hardly been a priority.

"Amelia Shaw?" Dr. Scarpa asked.

Amelia followed her inside. Her office was decorated in a much more clinical way than Jill's. No ostentatious art on the walls. No cozy furniture. The mood was completely different—almost austere.

They exchanged a few niceties before Dr. Scarpa cut to the chase. "Doctor Becket—I mean, Jill—emailed me earlier this week to disclose your relationship."

Amelia and Jill had agreed that Jill should be the one to inform her colleague. Jill had assured Amelia that was not a burden that should fall onto her. She also wanted to do her best to reduce any awkwardness between Amelia and her new therapist, because having to change mid-therapy was already awkward enough.

Amelia nodded. As far as she knew, Dr. Scarpa hadn't emailed Jill back to reassure her.

"I could pretend it never happens and that we psychiatrists are immune to developing feelings for our clients, but that would be untrue," Dr. Scarpa said. "I know Jill and I trust her judgment. It was good that she stopped treating you. That was the right thing to do."

"Yeah." Jill had asked Amelia to call her as soon as her first session was over, or to leave her a voicemail if she was in session. Not to break privilege, but just to let her know how Dr. Scarpa had reacted to the news of their relationship.

"How was it for you?" Dr. Scarpa asked. "To have to interrupt your treatment?"

"Well..." Amelia paused. "There are worse reasons to pause therapy for."

Dr. Scarpa stroked her chin. "I bet." She didn't look like the type that smiled too much, but she did manage a tight-lipped smile at that. "But don't make the mistake of confusing falling in love with healing. They might feel like the same thing, but they're not. We need to address the root causes for your burnout."

"Of course." Amelia remembered how, during the two and a half sessions they'd had together, she'd ranted at Jill about the state of the world and the general utter blah-ness of it all.

Dr. Scarpa might be very right. Falling in love was not the same as healing, yet Amelia felt a whole lot better regardless. Amelia knew it was down to a bunch of chemical reactions in her brain, but then again, her burnout had also been the result of a chemical reaction. Only this morning she'd been trying to find specific research on whether the feel-good chemicals of falling in love could counteract the detrimental effects of the relentless cortisol cycle that made a burnout so devastating to deal with. Unsurprisingly, she hadn't been able to find any research papers on the matter. Few serious scientists would consider researching something so frivolous as falling in love.

Amelia could be her very own study of one, although she knew very well that studies of only one person could never hold any scientific value. Nor was she going to run tests on samples of her own blood and saliva to prove a point. It was one of her greatest worries that she could come to rely on Jill for her mental well-being. But above all else, she also really wanted to enjoy the sensation of falling in love without overanalyzing it and correlating it to her burnout and the decrease in symptoms.

She paused before answering Dr. Scarpa. "Obviously, falling in love with Jill has made me feel a lot better about myself, but I'm very much aware of it, and awareness can be a great teacher. It's not only been great to fall in love, but it's been such a relief to feel something else than all the dread I've been submerged in for months. And the mere fact that I've been able to fall in love, which isn't something that I've previously allowed myself to do so easily, has been a bit of a revelation. Perhaps even a revolution."

"How so?" Dr. Scarpa didn't make any notes while she waited for a reply the way Jill did.

"Falling in love has never been easy for me. Partly because I've always put my job first, but also…" It was hard for Amelia to remember why it had been so difficult for her to surrender to another person's affection now that she was with Jill. "I don't know. Maybe that's something I can learn to articulate in here."

"Sure." Dr. Scarpa said. "Would you like to address that now or tackle the burnout first?"

Amelia could talk about Jill for days on end, but she didn't much feel like unearthing the patterns that underlay her life in romance. She didn't want to break the spell just yet. "I have been thinking about going back to work. Not to my old job. Let me rephrase that. I would like to go back to work and I would like that to coincide with a change of career."

"Any idea which direction you'd like to go?"

Dawn had mentioned teaching but Amelia didn't much feel like retraining so substantially, nor had she ever felt that particular kind of calling—and whenever Dawn talked about her job, it came across like a calling, how else could she put up with the negative aspects of it? "I have a few ideas, but it's still early days. I do see myself going back to work in the new year, so I can put this horror year behind me once and for all. Although"—her lips pulled into an inadvertent smile—"it hasn't all been bad, of course."

"But you feel ready to go out there again? When you picture yourself in an office or"—she looked at her so far unused notepad—"in the lab, that feels okay to you? What does it do to you physically when you actively visualize being at work again?"

"I can't imagine going back to my old job. I loved it for a long time, until I didn't. In fact, I've written my letter of resignation. I just need to email it." Amelia did feel a twinge of guilt toward her former boss and colleagues. Sending an email was so cold and distant. She should at least call or, if she felt herself capable—and maybe that was what she'd been waiting for—stop by her old place of work. "It's a chapter of my life I need to end, I know that much. It's time for something new."

"And to answer my question?" Dr. Scarpa nudged.

"To answer your question, if I get the job I'm thinking of applying for, then the only physical sensations generated when I imagine working there are a bunch of nerves and a humongous amount of excitement." Amelia hadn't told anyone—not Jill, not Dawn—about the change of career she was hoping for. She didn't want to get her own hopes up even higher by involving other people. And she suspected that any company or organization might think twice before hiring a new employee with a previous record of burnout, although she was fairly certain that, despite said burnout, she could get some excellent references from her soon-to-be-ex-employer.

"You're going to keep me in suspense?" Dr. Scarpa said, that almost-smile playing on her lips again.

"I just don't want to jinx it."

"Maybe we can talk about it next week?"

"Or the week after," Amelia said.

"Okay." Dr. Scarpa looked at her notepad again. "I read in the file that Jill sent me that you're crazy about soccer."

Crazy? Would Jill really have used that word to describe Amelia? Were psychiatrists even allowed to use it? Amelia made a mental note to quiz Jill on that later. The fact that she could, that after this session was over, she would go to Jill's house, where she could quiz—and kiss—her all she wanted, filled her with a warmth previously foreign to her.

"It's my hobby and I am, indeed, very passionate about it." Amelia had, semi-successfully, tried to get Jill excited about the English Premier League, which was her own favorite. Any further attempts to recruit her for the Darlinghurst Darlings had been met with hysterical laughter. Jill was the type of woman who looked her best with a flute of Champagne in her hand rather than a ball at her foot, although Amelia believed she could convince her that one didn't have to exclude the other. "I've put myself forward to take on some more responsibility." Amelia had had a chat with Kate to discuss whether she could become assistant-coach, to which Kate had replied that if Amelia wanted to coach the team so badly, she was very welcome to the job of first and only coach.

"I do love Sam Kerr," Dr. Scarpa said.

"Sam Kerr is a f—" Amelia stopped herself from swearing in her brand-new therapist's office. "She's a legend." And one of the reasons Amelia subscribed to an expensive European soccer TV package. If Amelia was experiencing any doubts at all about resuming her therapy with Dr. Scarpa, her admission of loving Sam Kerr was more than enough to dissolve any remaining ones.

Chapter Thirty-Three

TWO MONTHS LATER

Jill had no idea what she was doing, nor how she had ended up on a soccer pitch, dressed in skimpy shorts and a too-tight jersey. She looked behind her. Amelia was gazing out over the pitch, focused on the position of the ball. Speaking of, where was the ball? Jill should probably keep an eye on it as well, seeing that she was playing in defense. But even if she did, it wouldn't make any difference to the team. She was just here to make up the numbers, because who in their right mind wanted to compete in a soccer tournament on Boxing Day? Amelia Shaw, that's who.

Amelia now had such sway over Jill that she had, firstly, convinced her to join the Darlinghurst Darlings and, secondly, persuaded her to play in the tournament. As a psychiatrist, she instinctively knew this wasn't right. Yes, Jill was absolutely crazy about Amelia, but she'd never in a million years imagined herself doing this—playing soccer and thus making a fool of herself—for another woman.

"Jill," Amelia shouted from behind her. "Look out!"

Amelia took her new role as coach of the Darlings extremely seriously—this, apparently, included raising her voice at everyone on the team, including her own girlfriend. A player of the opposite team dribbled toward the goal. Jill had to do something to stop her. Amelia had tried to teach her how to tackle an opponent—always play the ball, never the woman—but Jill had not taken to it. It required her body to make a sliding motion that simply didn't come naturally to her. Jill should be stealing leftover turkey from the fridge, not trying to stop a woman from shooting at Amelia's goal.

Half-heartedly, she ran toward the other team's forward. It wasn't the first time Jill had tried to stop her during this game. Luckily, the Darlings had two other defenders, who picked up all of Jill's slack. Earlier, after Amelia had made a save, she had told Jill that it was all right. Nobody had high expectations of her during her very first game, especially with her non-existent soccer background.

Still, Jill tried to make an effort. She tried to at least put her body in front of the other player, but the woman was very fast and agile with the ball. How was it even possible to control a round object with your feet like that? It defied all laws of physics. But that it was very much possible was currently impossible to ignore. Soccer was big business all around the world, a fact that Jill enjoyed needling Amelia about.

"For someone who likes to rant about the evils of capitalism, you sure don't have the same complaints about soccer, darling," Jill had said while Amelia was watching a game the other day.

"Some things bring too much joy to spend energy on rants about them," Amelia had simply replied. She had effectively shut Jill up with one single sentence, which was also due to the fact that Jill wanted nothing more than for Amelia to experience maximum joy in her life. If there was one activity that brought her joy, it was soccer. Hence Jill's presence on this very soccer pitch.

There was no chance in hell she'd be catching the other team's player.

"Oh, bugger," she heard Hera say from a few meters away. They both looked on as Amelia came out of her goal to either heroically stop the ball from entering her goal or, if she didn't succeed, say goodbye to keeping a clean sheet. Amelia slid forward, forcing the forward to make her final move. She tried to lob the ball over Amelia, who managed to swat it away thanks to her long arms.

Unlike Jill, Hera ran toward the goal to try to recapture the ball before the opposite team tried scoring again. Of course, Jill wanted the Darlings to win, but she wasn't entirely sure how much she was willing to break into a sweat to help this happen.

"Go, Hera," Katherine shouted from the sideline. Seeing her there, all glammed up as usual, made Jill wonder again what she was doing on the pitch instead of cheering on the Darlings from the side. She only had to cast another glance at Amelia to know the reason. The woman was so damn persuasive, Jill simply couldn't say no. She should address this with Vic, before it turned into an actual problem. But Amelia was in her element amongst her team. So, of course Jill had wanted to join, if only to see how she behaved surrounded by her teammates.

Jill watched as Hera retrieved the ball. Their gazes locked across the distance. Oh, no. Hera kicked the ball toward her. Jill didn't even have time to take a breath. She caught the ball awkwardly against her hip, off which it bounced, and landed a few feet away from her.

"Go on then, Jill," a woman shouted from the sideline, but Jill had no time to check who it was. She had to do something with the ball before the other team took it from her and assailed Amelia's goal again. She sprinted toward the ball and, once there, glanced around to spot an available Darling to pass it to. Sheryl was only a few feet ahead of her, shouting for Jill to pass her the ball. How could she be eager for it? She'd joined the Darlings at the same time as Jill. Unlike Jill she had taken to it like a duck to water, although, by her own admission, her level of physical fitness left a lot to be desired. Jill couldn't get rid of the ball in her possession quickly enough—which probably wasn't the right attitude to have on a soccer pitch—so she passed it to Sheryl, only for it to end up in the feet of an opponent. Oh well. She had tried. If the coach wanted to give her an earful for another botched-up pass, Jill knew how to deal with that. She would tackle her straight onto the bed and kiss her until she shut up.

Before the other team could make another dash at Amelia's goal, the ref blew the whistle for half-time. Dawn jogged up to Jill.

"Are you having fun?" she asked.

"Maybe fun is not the right word for it."

"I know the coach pretty well." Dawn grinned at her. "I can put in a good word to have you substituted in the second half."

For this Boxing Day match, the Darlings had only one substitute player on the bench who, according to Amelia—and said to Jill in the strictest confidence during pillow talk last night—had the least natural ability with a football Amelia had ever witnessed. She did attract the most attention, however, even while sitting on the bench.

"Hey," Amelia took Jill aside for a second. "Sorry for shouting earlier."

"Don't worry about it. Things get said in the heat of the game. I understand."

"How are you holding up?" Amelia asked while taking off her gloves.

"More than ready to be substituted," Jill admitted.

"Okay." They walked into the locker room together. "Time to throw Caitlin James to the lions."

Chapter Thirty-Four

"To the Darlinghurst Darlings!" Amelia raised her glass to her teammates gathered in the pub after the game.

Usually, after a loss, she'd be much more down in the dumps, but it was the day after Christmas and these women had shown up for her—that was what it felt like, anyway. Even Jill had donned the Darlings' kit and tried her best. The team had welcomed four new members, with varying degrees of ability, but that could be worked on. In the end, they only played for fun. Even though she was the coach now, Amelia could see her team for what it truly was: a bunch of women coming together to have some good old-fashioned fun. And she'd be able to use her knowledge of soccer in the professional arena soon enough. A surge of excitement ran through her at the prospect. She started her new job next week.

"Maybe I would be better as a forward," Caitlin said. "Defense doesn't really seem to suit me."

"Maybe you'd be better as the PR person," Sheryl said. "Mouthing off next to the pitch instead of all the moaning you do on it." She flashed Caitlin a smile.

Personality-wise, Amelia liked the new additions to the Darlings. Sheryl and Caitlin had known each other forever and—even Amelia wasn't immune to this—Caitlin did bring a touch of glamour to the team. Hera, although in her fifties, had been a soccer revelation. It had been seeing Hera play that had convinced Amelia to not start her own 40+ team, because women like Hera—and like herself—could still add so much value to a team like the Darlings, despite their mature age.

Amelia knew that Jill had only joined the team to please her, making her the most likely new team member to be the first to quit. But Hera had told Amelia that, come the new year, she believed her 'very sporty' friend Liz might try out for the team as well. Now that the Darlings had some new blood, Amelia fully believed in the team again. Now that she was the coach, she could hardly feel like her position on the team was in danger. In hindsight, Amelia could even see that her position had never been up for discussion at all. It was her brain playing tricks on her, casting everything in a dark veil of doom. A veil that had started to lift once she had started therapy and had gradually disintegrated into what was barely a translucent layer of almost-nothingness.

"Once you start your fancy new job," Dawn said to Amelia, "you'll be able to transform us into near-pro-level players."

"Amelia's a scientist," Hera said, "not a magician."

They all broke out into laughter.

"I'll do nothing but my best for you," Amelia said, meaning it from the bottom of her heart. Dawn's allusion to her new job made something in her stomach clench. It wasn't only excitement mixed with inevitable nerves. It was the simple fact of having a job, of being able to go back to work fully energized, ready to tackle the day, to get back into a routine. To be a functioning person in society—albeit still the same old capitalist one—again. Although, of course, Amelia had no idea how she would feel once she was on the job. On paper, it sounded like it had been created especially for her: a soccer-mad scientist.

After the new year, she would begin a brand-new career as a sports scientist for a professional club, Sydney Football Club. She would use her knowledge of biochemistry and her love for analytics to make both the male and female teams perform better. Getting the job was like a dream come true. It meant soccer and science during work hours and soccer and Jill after hours. Amelia couldn't even have dreamed up a life like that.

"Don't start neglecting us because we're only amateurs," Sheryl said.

"The Darlings will always be my first love," Amelia said.

"Good to know, darling." Jill put her hand on Amelia's knee.

"Soccer-wise, I mean." Amelia quickly kissed Jill on the cheek. In response, Jill leaned into her.

"A shout-out to Jill, ladies," Hera raised her glass. "For surviving her first game."

"To be honest, it might be my last." Jill bumped her shoulder against Amelia's. "Sorry, darling. I'm not sure it's for me. I'm not competitive enough."

"Yes, that's probably the main issue," Hera said.

"Not my issue at all," Caitlin said. "But the other team's players were just so damn fast."

"I think it was more that you were a bit slow," Sheryl said.

"What do you think, coach?" Hera asked. "Will you draw up a personal fitness schedule for each of us? Going for a run three times a week and things like that?"

"Just show up for practice and every single one of you will automatically improve," Amelia said.

"If you're so keen to improve your fitness," Dawn said. "I have two kids at home who require a lot of running around after. Everyone's very welcome at our house any time for an advanced fitness session."

"Maybe Amber can teach a class in post-match yoga," Kristin said.

Amelia listened to her team's banter—because the Darlinghurst Darlings felt like *her* team again—with a wide smile on her face. Jill's hand was still on her knee.

In a few days, on New Year's Eve, she would have someone to kiss passionately at the stroke of midnight. Someone she would wake up next to on the first day of the new year—a new year that could only be infinitely better than the last. The next Monday she would start her brand-new job. The weekend after her first week at her new dream job, the Darlings would be playing against the current leaders of the league. Amelia wouldn't be surprised if, against all odds, they'd start the new year with a big win. Because that was how it felt since she and Jill had kissed the first time, even though she'd still had alarm bells going off in her head: as though the odds had turned in her favor again. As though everything was possible again, the very opposite feeling to what she'd experienced for the better part of the past year.

She curled her arms around Jill, leaned into her, and found her ear. "Thanks for playing for my team," she whispered.

"You do know you can make me do anything you want," Jill said. "If you ask me in that sultry voice of yours."

"Good to know," Amelia whispered in Jill's ear, making sure her voice dipped into its lowest register possible.

Acknowledgments

Dear Reader,

Here we are, at the end of the 10th book in the Pink Bean series and (depending on when you're reading this) at the end of this very strange year 2020.

For Caroline and me it was supposed to be a huge year of celebrations. We met in 2000 and have been together 20 years of which we've been married 10. We were going to travel and party and whatnot, but of course we didn't do any of these things.

As I write this, at the height of the second lockdown in Belgium, even I, the mega-introvert and person who can go a very long time without social interactions, can't wait to see people again. But these are the times we live in and this, too, will pass.

In the end, despite feeling decidedly *bleurgh* from time to time (a feeling we are all entitled to, no matter our circumstances), I do know I'm very lucky.

Even though we didn't get to go on our dream holiday, my wife and I did celebrate our 10th wedding anniversary, we just did it at home (with the real winner of the lock-down: our cat, Dolly Purrton.)

Being confined to the house has allowed me to write a lot this year and produce a few books that will mean the world to me forever. I was able to release my 30th published novel (*A Breathless Place*) to such warm reviews and maybe, without having to go so inward because of the lockdown, I might not have been able to write a book like that.

And, of course, two years after Pink Bean 9 was released, I finally started on Pink Bean 10! It has been a long time coming and I wanted it to be warm and sexy but relatively drama-free. I wanted it to celebrate friendships and the coziness of coffee shops and completely ignore the coronavirus. I just wanted you to be able to escape into a familiar world and have a good time. What better means to accomplish that than a return to the Pink Bean? To Sheryl and Kristin and Caitlin and Jo and Liz and Jess and all the others. It has certainly lifted my spirits to be able to do so.

In this difficult year, the return to the familiar mixed with two new characters (while taking rather large artistic liberties with my representation of how real-life therapists behave ;-0) is my gift to you. You reading this is your very kind gift to me, so: thank you very much!

As always, I must thank my wife, who has been by my side for twenty years now. We've had so many adventures during those two decades and I'm sure we'll have many more. The amount of encouragement she has given me during the past twenty years, but especially during this last one, is immeasurable. (And how absolutely gorgeous are the new covers she made for the entire Pink Bean series?)

Then, there's my friend and editor Cheyenne Blue, who first edited one of my books (*At the Water's Edge*) in 2014, when I was still only a Cheyenne Blue fan-girl-from-a-distance. Six years down the line, she has edited 90% of my novels and I'm so grateful for the connection this has created between us. Cheyenne is such an amazing editor who always, so expertly, walks that fine line between being too harsh and too friendly. That our friendship has survived for so long is the truest testament to that.

Enormous gratitude to Claire Jarrett, who proofreads my books and who has also made detailed summaries of all Pink Bean books and character sheets for every single character. Without this, it would have been impossible for me to write Pink Bean 10 two years after Pink Bean 9 was released.

My trusted beta-reader, Carrie Camp, always gives me her gut instinct when first reading my books, which is something I've come to rely on to make the final version the best it can be. (Carrie also sent me a wonderful bottle of wine during lockdown, a much-appreciated act of friendship as well as a tasty introduction to Texan wine.)

Thank you, as always, to my Launch Team, of which some of the members have been on the team for years and years. Endless thanks for reading my books early and giving me your honest feedback.

As always—last but definitely not least!—thank you to you, the reader. Your continued support is what has allowed me to write and publish so many books over the years and it has also made 2020 bearable on quite a few levels.

A special shout-out to those of you who interact with me in my Facebook group and provide chuckles when I need them most (you can really never go wrong with a cat gif.)

To those of you who have emailed me to say you really enjoyed one of my books. To those of you who reached out after reading *A Breathless Place* to either ask whether I was doing okay (I was and am, but I understand the question) or to share your own story. Especially during these strange times, I have become a strong believer in sharing and getting a message from you always cheers me up.

I also explicitly want to thank those readers who simply read and never get in touch but make up the vast majority of my readership. Thank you so much for giving me the continued opportunity to do what I love the most: write about two women falling in love.

Thank you,

Harper xo

About the Author

Harper Bliss is a best-selling lesbian romance author. Among her most-loved books are the highly dramatic French Kissing and the often thought-provoking Pink Bean series.

Harper lived in Hong Kong for 7 years, travelled the world for a bit, and has now settled in Brussels (Belgium) with her wife and photogenic cat, Dolly Purrton.

Together with her wife, she hosts a weekly podcast called Harper Bliss & Her Mrs.

Harper loves hearing from readers and you can reach her at the email address below.

www.harperbliss.com
harper@harperbliss.com

Printed in Great Britain
by Amazon